D1527796

THE
RULE OF THREE

EXTINCTION NZ BOOK 1

ADRIAN J SMITH

GREAT WAVE INK
PUBLISHING

GREAT WAVE INK
PUBLISHING

This book is for my mother,
who encouraged me to read from an early age
Thank you for the gift of imagination.

Also, to all those who experience bullying.

Hope is being able to see
That there is light despite
All of the darkness
–Desmond Tutu

Acknowledgements

First, I would like to again take this opportunity to thank Nicholas Sansbury Smith for encouraging me to write in his Extinction Cycle world. You continue to amaze and inspire me every day. Thank you so much.

To Frances, thank you for your words of encouragement and reading every single draft.

To Nathan, for reading an early draft and making some vital suggestions, thank you.

To Rodger for your humour and keeping me sane. Barbara and Phyl, thank you for reading the first draft, and for your encouragement.

To the Street Team, you guys are awesome. Thank you so much for your friendship.

To all my Beta readers, Lisa, Bill, Michael, thank you. To Col (Ret) Olson and author Steve Konkoly for your invaluable military RT input, and Susan for your medical advice. If you find any mistakes, they are entirely my fault.

To Laurel, you deserve a huge thank you for taking a rough pile of notes and turning them into something readable.

Most importantly, thanks to the readers for taking a chance and reading my novel set in the Extinction universe created by Nicholas Sansbury Smith. I wanted to tell a story from a New Zealand point of view set in this world and I tried to imagine what would happen if an everyman and everywoman were caught up in an apocalypse.

We are a small nation with a small, but determined and proud, armed force. We have stood by our British, Australian and American brothers in times of war. As a whole, we don't have a lot of firearms readily available, but they are there, mainly for hunting purposes.

Because this book is set in New Zealand, I have used UK spelling and there are some Kiwi phrases. If any of them confuse you, please email me for an explanation.

All the place names and locations in this book are real, and I encourage you to look them up on Google Maps. Or better yet, come and visit our beautiful country. Perhaps I'll take you hiking.

Fate is a theme in this book, and it is indeed a funny thing, because it was fate that led me to the Extinction Cycle via another book in 2015. Reaching out to Nicholas led me to a great friendship and his amazing books. Which has now led me to write my first book.

I would be eternally grateful if you could leave an honest review when finishing the book. Doing so will help me develop as a writer.

Thanks again for reading. Be sure to look out for the next adventures of Jack, Dee and Boss.

Cheers
Adrian

Foreword
by
Nicholas Sansbury Smith

Dear Reader,

Thank you for picking up a copy of The Rule of Three by Adrian Smith. This is the first of a planned trilogy documenting Jack Gee and his struggle to survive in a post-apocalyptic New Zealand. Originally published through Amazon's Extinction Cycle Kindle World, The Rule of Three became a reader favourite in the Extinction Cycle series side stories, and transcended to far more than fan fiction. Unfortunately, Amazon ended the Kindle Worlds program in July of 2018 with little warning. Authors were given a chance to republish or retire their stories, and I jumped at the chance to republish The Rule of Three through my small press, Great Wave Ink. Today, we're proud to offer T Rule of Three in paperback, audio, and to readers outside of the United States for the first time ever.

For those of you that are new to the Extinction Cycle storyline, the series is the award winning, Amazon top-rated, and half a million copy best-selling seven book saga. There are over six *thousand* five-star reviews on Amazon alone. Critics have called it, "World War Z and The Walking Dead meets the Hot Zone." Publishers weekly added, "Smith has realised that the way to rekindle interest in zombie apocalypse fiction is to make it louder, longer, and bloodier... Smith intensifies the disaster efficiently as the pages flip by, and readers who enjoy juicy blood-and-guts action will find a lot of it here."

In creating the Extinction Cycle, my goal was to use authentic military action and real science to take the zombie and post-apocalyptic genres in an exciting new direction. Forget everything you know about zombies. In the Extinction Cycle, they aren't created by black magic or other supernatural means. The ones found in the Extinction Cycle are created by a military bio-weapon called VX-99, first used in Vietnam. The chemicals reactivate the proteins encoded by the genes that separate humans from wild animals—in other words, the experiment turned men into monsters. For the first time, zombies are explained using real science—science so real there is every possibility of something like the Extinction Cycle actually happening. But these creatures aren't the unthinking, slow-minded, shuffling monsters we've all come to know in other shows, books, and movies. These "variants" are more monster than human. Through the series, the variants become the hunters as they evolve from the epigenetic changes. Scrambling to find a cure and defeat the monsters, humanity is brought to the brink of extinction.

We hope you enjoy The Rule of Three and continue on with the rest of the Extinction NZ series, and the main storyline in the Extinction Cycle. Thank you for reading!

Best wishes,
Nicholas Sansbury Smith,
USA Today Bestselling Author of the Extinction Cycle

Prologue

Three weeks without food...

Jack's fevered mind chanted it like a Buddhist mantra, over and over. The proverbial rule of three. Problem was, Jack had no idea how long he'd been here. When they scampered around, their bones and joints made strange, popping sounds. And when they came to harvest their human captives, their weird mouths made a sucking, smacking noise, like a child eating an ice cream on a hot day. Jack hated that sound. And the stench they exuded was disgusting, a rotten fruit smell. It reminded him of the Durian fruit he had tried once in a Thai market, in a happier time before hell had descended on Earth.

Three days without water...

The agony of the deep gash in Jack's thigh kept him semi-conscious with moments of lucidity. Occasional screams cut through the warm damp air, jolting him fully conscious. His eyes would snap open and blink rapidly as he hoped that his predicament had changed, but the surrounding darkness and environment remained the same.

Jack was stuck fast to a wall with some sort of gluey membrane. He struggled against it in sheer terror and panic. He could only move his arms and legs a few measly inches, no matter how hard he fought. Each time he managed to stay awake for a few minutes, he would strain against his bonds, but whatever it was that held him, it had the strength of steel.

Three hours without shelter...

A humming sound in the background reminded Jack of high-powered electric lines, while the cold, damp hardness of concrete pushed into the back of his legs and head, chilling him to the bone. The constant scurrying, and the smacking sounds the creatures made, haunted his fragile psyche, making him flinch whenever he heard them. Never a religious man, Jack found himself praying to any higher power he could think of. *There are no atheists in a foxhole. Well, what about down here in the dark?*

Three minutes without air...

Twisting his left arm back and forth, and scraping skin off in the process, Jack could almost reach the valve of his water bladder. Miraculously, his hiking pack was still on his shoulders. With a final effort, Jack grasped the valve in his hand. Bending his arm and pushing his head as far forwards as he could, Jack was agonisingly close to that life-saving liquid. He bellowed in frustration.

A popping sound alerted Jack to the monsters'

approach. He cursed at his stupidity. Holding his breath and keeping his body rigid, Jack squeezed his eyes shut.

Not me not me not me not me...

The rotten fruit smell lingered as the creatures carried out their grotesque task. Jack kept his eyes closed and forced himself to breathe in shallow breaths. He listened as he heard a tearing sound, followed by the sickening thud of a body hitting the ground. The monsters clicked at each other in some sort of communication. Jack gritted his teeth and screamed in silent terror as the popping of their joints faded away.

Not me not me not me...it's not me...it's not me this time.

— 1 —

Jack gazed up at the stars, captivated by the serenity and majesty of the little pinpricks of light. As many times as he looked at the Milky Way, he never grew bored with it. He would spend hours searching out the constellations he knew, trying to name them.

Scorpius.

Canis Major.

The Southern Cross.

And a cluster of stars New Zealanders liked to call "The Pot". Jack had been meaning to find out what its correct name was, but he'd never got around to it. Recently he had learnt about Pleiades, or what the Maori called Matariki, but he didn't bother searching for that cluster of stars now. It only appeared from late May or early June.

He inhaled deeply, the fresh forest scents lacing the chill air. He loved it up here in the mountains, away from the rat race. As much as he loved technology, with its smartphones, flat screen TVs, computers, and all conceivable gadgets, all to make humanities wander through time easier, the wilderness was where he felt at peace, at home. Jack smirked. An eternal conflict.

When he thought about it, it was the silence he liked. That, and being able to see the galaxy spread across the night sky. In the wilderness, it was just him and nature. Nothing but the echoes of the stars. For three days he had enjoyed being off the grid. For three days he had let his mind wander. He had played out his favourite movie scenes in his head. Laughed. Cried at memories as he stepped one foot in front of the other. Through mud. Over tree roots. Often Jack had to duck under branches and squeeze through fallen trees. For kilometre after kilometre he had been at peace.

His wife, Dee, would often ask him why he liked to hike alone. The only answer he could ever come up with was: *It's like being a nomad again. Being one with yourself.*

When he'd arrived at the hut earlier in the evening, he'd resisted the urge to make contact with Dee for as long as possible. He sighed and stretched out his knotted shoulders. He took one last look at the stars. Digging reluctantly into his pack, he pulled out his phone. It was time to reconnect and let her know he was okay.

Immediately after booting up, it alerted him to several messages. Looking at the screen, Jack saw that they were all from Dee, the first sent three days ago. He spent a few minutes scanning through them.

Jack. Call me…

Please call me it's urgent…

For Pete's sake Jack!

Something weird is going on. Please call…

Jack frowned. He opened the last one.

Jack there's been a virus outbreak in America. It's

spreading fast. Please call me and tell me you're okay. I'm worried baby. This sounds serious. xoxo

He gasped. *Really? A virus? Is this a joke?*

Pushing the phone icon, he held his breath as the phone rang. It sounded distant and garbled. After what seemed like minutes, Dee answered.

"Jack? Thank God!" Without letting him answer, she continued, "Listen, it's all over the news. They've closed all the airports, all the ports, everything is closing or closed down. You need to get home now, please, Jack. It's horrible, it's crazy, it's…"

"Dee, slow down. What's going on?"

"It's some virus in the States. It started in Chicago. It's already been reported in London, Paris, Sydney…everywhere!"

"Okay, so we go to the cabin and wait it out. We prepared for this."

"It gets worse, Jack."

"How?"

"There are rumours about it turning people into monsters."

From the panic in Dee's voice, Jack knew she was serious.

"Monsters? How?"

"Who knows. All I saw was blurry footage on the news. They want everyone to stay inside. Lock your doors."

"What about Civil Defence?" Jack said, his eyes scrunching together. "What are they saying?"

"Same thing. Stay indoors. Wait."

Jack pulled the phone away from his ear and looked

out over the dark mountains.

Had they had finally done it? What so many people had imagined? Had they killed the world?

Whoever "they" were.

Was it true? Had the end of the world come? A virus outbreak? Monsters?

So many thoughts swam through his head. He loved movies, comics and sci fi. Jack had daydreamed about this sort of thing happening plenty of times. He had even convinced Dee to get an isolated cabin in the woods for this kind of eventuality.

But that was just a fantasy, right? This sort of thing doesn't really happen, does it?

"Jack? Are you there? Babe!" Dee's voice cut through his thoughts. "You have to come home. I need you."

He looked at his phone, struggling to grasp what was happening. He took a couple of deep breaths, letting the air out of his lungs slowly. Finally, he held the phone back to his ear. "I don't think the city will be safe for long. If the virus reaches New Zealand, it'll turn bad, and fast. What about our cabin?"

"I think it's already here. Th…There've been conflicting reports of it in Auckland." Dee paused. Jack could just picture her running a hand through her hair as she sat on the couch, her legs tucked under her petite frame. "Come home, baby. We'll pick up your mother and head to the cabin."

"Okay. Good idea." He was thinking fast now. "Call her and let her know what's happening. Fill up as much water as possible into any available container, get our bug-out bags, and gather as much food as you can." Jack smiled. "Dee?"

"Yeah?"

"I love you. I'll see you in a few hours."

"Love you too, baby. Hurry!"

"Okay." Jack's phone crackled. "And lock up!" He spent a few seconds watching the reception bars on the screen, waiting for them to come back on, but they remained blank. After a moment, the 'no signal' icon flashed.

Jack pivoted and looked over to Mt Te Aroha. It was only four kilometres away and he could clearly see the tall communications tower that dominated the skyline. He should have perfect reception.

Grumbling to himself, Jack slipped the phone into his pocket.

Emptying out his pack, he found his headlamp. His heart pounded in his chest, and he could feel the tension building, like a violinist playing strained and suspenseful music. He hurried over to fill his water bladder up at the basin, catching his reflection in the mirror as he did so. He ran a hand through his dark hair and couldn't help but notice the worried look in his blue eyes.

Pack light, for we travel far and swift.

Glancing over his trail map one last time, he decided to take the shorter but steeper track down to the car park. *This is going to be a tough hike*, thought Jack as he slammed the hut door behind him.

Jogging down the trail, he thought back to the day he and Dee had met.

It was the height of summer. A hazy glare bounced off the trees in the valley, and Jack could see and smell the pollen coming off the poplar trees. Taking a breath, Jack heard two excited voices coming up the trail, the roar of the waterfall and the gurgling of the stream no match for the high-pitched excitement. Looking, he saw her for the first time. Petite, pixie-cut brown hair, bright blue eyes and a gorgeous smile. And when she turned towards him, he could see a tattoo of flowers creeping up her arm.

Jack turned away shyly, but still managed to smile at her.

Enjoying his lunch, he listened as the two girls took in the view, snapped photos and chatted. He was pleased when they sat close by to eat their lunch.

He was readying himself to leave when he felt the air change. "Do you know how far that trail goes?"

The voice was almost sing-song, its sweet tones music to his ears.

Jack looked in the direction Pixie-hair was pointing. "As far north as north goes."

Pixie-hair laughed. "Isn't it 'as far south as south goes'?"

Jack smiled. "Yeah, but I know nothing."

She stuck out her hand. "I'm Diana, but my friends call me Dee."

Jack grinned, his cheeks hurting. "James, but everyone calls me Jack."

It was hard going. Down, down, down. He hated down. His knee joints ground with every step. He could feel the lactic acid building. He gritted his teeth. He picked his way over the gnarled tree roots that twisted over the trail and dodged granite boulders. He hurried past evidence of the area's gold mining past. Boilers and steam compressors rusting away in their steel frames. Other relics sat amongst the undergrowth, all but forgotten. Jack ignored it all. His focus was on Dee. On getting down from these mountains safely. As he jogged down the trail, he could hear the hoot of owls, the squawks of kakariki and the coos of wood pigeons as they searched for their meals. Normally he would stop and watch them, fascinated by their routine. Not tonight. The trail finally flattened out as he came up to the swing bridge. Without even glancing at the view, Jack jogged on.

Only one more hour.

Those countless times he'd hiked this trail were really helping him in the darkness.

Forty minutes later he arrived at the car park. He fumbled for his keys as he ran up to his SUV. Finally getting them in hand, he unlocked the door, slung his backpack onto the passenger seat and jumped in. Jamming the key into the ignition, he started the engine, whacked it into gear and sped off, tyres spinning in the loose gravel.

I'm coming, darling. I'm nearly there.

With one hand on the wheel, he turned on his phone, tapped the phone icon and put it on speaker. Nothing but garbled sound emitted from it. Looking at the bars, Jack swore in frustration. *"CRAP! SHITTY SHIT!"*

He leant over and turned the volume up on the car stereo. A strange monotone beep filled the silence. Frowning, he scanned through all the FM stations. Nothing. His pulse quickening, Jack switched to AM, and heard an emergency broadcast. He listened to it a few times but got no actual details of the virus. It was just the announcer advising people to stay indoors. Jack ran a sweaty hand through his hair. Letting out a breath, he turned the radio off in frustration.

— 2 —

Jack sped through the night, the road dipping as it followed the undulating countryside. He kept off the main roads, taking the narrower but straighter roads that dissected the flat farmland. His eyes scanned the houses as he flew past, searching for signs of life. Every house was dark; people had either left or the power was off.

Jack grimaced at each dark building he saw and fought the urge to drive faster. The closer he got to Hamilton, the more his trepidation grew. After thirty minutes of speeding his way along the back roads, Jack decided to risk the highway, his worry for Dee and his family making up his mind.

As soon as he turned onto the main road he spotted an orange glow up ahead. His mind flashed back to his time in Australia. A glow like that normally meant a fire. Slowing his car, he wound down the window. Acrid smoke wafted in, making him cough. *Definitely fire.*

Jack dropped his speed further and glanced in his rearview mirror, searching behind for any vehicles, in case he needed to make a quick U-turn. The glow intensified as he rounded a sharp bend, and before him was the cause of the fire. He jammed on the brakes.

Cars lined the road on both sides, their occupants milling around. About 100 metres away, he could see a jack-knifed milk tanker strewn across the road, its ends tangled in fences on both sides. It was engulfed in flames, thick black smoke pouring out over the land.

Alongside him, on the shoulder of the road, a family sat waiting in an old mini-van.

Winding his window right down, he made eye contact with the driver. "Hey, been waiting long?"

"About an hour," replied the man.

Jack could see him quite well in the light from the blaze. He looked about 40 and had on a flat cap, like the English wear — or the hipsters. The woman sitting alongside had her hands over her ears. Hearing the bickering of kids from the back seat, he could understand why.

Jack turned his attention back to Flatcap. "Any sign of the emergency services?"

"Nope, not yet. It's pretty crazy out there. The roads are jammed up."

"Because of the virus?"

"Yeah. They announced it on the news, told everyone to stay home from work, only essential travel. That was yesterday. We decided to go and stay with family, get out of Auckland. I guess everyone else had the same idea."

"What about Hamilton?"

"Couldn't get past the Bombay Hills. The police directed us onto this road."

Jack nodded, contemplating the new information. Looking out at the tanker, the fire raging out of control and all the cars jammed up, he knew that if he was to get home to Dee, he'd have to go the long way around.

Making his decision, he turned back to Flatcap. "Thanks mate. I'm going to try a different way. I really need to get home to my wife." He revved the car up and shifted it into gear.

"Hey!" called out Flatcap.

"Yeah?"

"Can you give us directions?"

"Sure, where are you headed?"

"Cambridge."

"Cambridge? Okay. Follow me. I'll show you to the turn off."

The lady, who had not uttered a sound until now, turned and looked at Jack. "Thank you. It's madness out there."

A high-pitched scream echoed through the night. Jack and Flatcap exchanged a look.

Squinting into the glare from the fire, Jack could just make out the source of screaming. A couple were running down the road towards where he was stopped, terror sharpening their features. The woman let out another primal scream as a black blur slammed into her. They went down in a tangled mess of arms and legs, just a few car lengths away. The black blur had stopped above them and came into focus.

Jack stared. He was having trouble comprehending what his eyes were seeing. It looked like a monster straight out of his worst nightmares.

The creature looked human enough. Or like something that had once been human. Its limbs had elongated, and where its feet and hands should have been, were claws. Large yellow eyes stared back at Jack. They blinked, as if the creature was deciding whether to attack him or finish off the woman. The monster glared at Jack and shrieked.

Jack's heart hammered in his chest, sending a shot of adrenaline right through his body. He struggled to think straight. The creature crouched over the woman. Jack watched, dazed, as it plunged its head down and tore out the woman's throat. Spurts of arterial blood coated the creature's face, the plasma glowing a hellish red in the firelight. It turned its head towards Jack, as though it could see him watching, and it licked its strange, sucker-like lips. Then letting out a horrible screech, it returned to its meal.

Jack's hands started to shake but he was unable to look away despite the horror.

The creature was reptilian-looking with blackish translucent skin. Where the mouth should have been was a weird sucker-like appendage filled with sharp teeth. Jack squeezed his eyes shut, trying to block out the image, but it was seared into his mind.

A cacophony of sounds echoed through his head. Shouts and screams. Engines starting. The swoosh of blood pumped through his ears. Frantic cries of terrified children. Children!

Snapping out of it, Jack looked back towards Flatcap's car. Flatcap's children were screaming.

Throwing his car into reverse, Jack screamed, "C'mon!"

But the crashing sound of glass breaking made him stop. Terrified screams pierced the night.

To his horror, three more of the creatures had appeared out of the smoke and chaos and were swarming all over Flatcap's car. One of them reached in through the shattered windshield — that must have been the breaking glass he'd heard — and dragged the woman out by her hair. Before he could consider the consequences, he put his car into drive and barrelled towards the creature.

Jack sideswiped it, flinging it backwards several metres and smashing it into another vehicle. The creature shook its head groggily, glared at him, and let out a horrific shriek.

"Get in!" Jack yelled at the woman, all the time keeping his eyes on the monster.

She whimpered, but hauled herself up with steely determination and jumped into Jack's car.

"Go! Go!" Jack shouted out the window at Flatcap. Two of the creatures were still on top of his car.

Flatcap managed to get his car moving and expertly spun the wheels despite the loose gravel on the shoulder of the road. Wrenching the car side to side, he came out of the melee, throwing the two monsters off and into the ditch in the process.

Flooring the accelerator again, Jack squealed back down the road.

I'll find you, Dee. Just stay put. I'm coming, promise.

"Holy shit, what the hell was THAT?" Jack said, more to himself than to his passenger. A cold sweat enveloped him. Images of what he'd just witnessed flashed through his mind. He tried to calm himself.

Deep breaths, in, out, in, out, in out. Deep breaths…

Though Jack could see Flatcap's car up ahead, he was struggling to keep up with his panicked driving. Both cars tore through the night. He focused on the red tail lights, following his driving lines.

"What the hell was that?"

He barely heard the quiet response. "Dante's bloody inferno."

Jack nodded his head in agreement. "Did you see its mouth?"

"Yeah."

He looked over at his passenger. She had her hands in her lap. He could see by the way she leant away from him, curled against the back of her seat, that she wanted to be left alone with her thoughts. Staring out the windscreen, focussing on the road, Jack had time to think.

He just couldn't make sense of it. What the hell were those things he'd just seen? Were they what people became if they caught this virus? That just didn't make any kind of sense. Outside of science fiction, that is. Surely no one had managed to create a virus that turned people into monsters? Surely? He shook his head. He had so many questions, and no answers. He banged the steering wheel in anger.

Stay safe, Dee. I'm coming.

Jack looked down at his shaky, sweaty hands. He wiped them on his pants in turn, trying to dry them. He clenched them into fists to try to stop the shaking, gripping and regripping the steering wheel as he did so. His mind just kept replaying the horrifying creature tearing out the poor woman's throat and lapping up her blood.

The car shuddered and swerved as it went over onto the gravel shoulder, threatening to skid out. Jack cringed, cursing at himself as he watched a road sign go under the front of the car. He took his foot off the accelerator and pulled the steering wheel hard down to the right. To his relief, he regained control of the car. The car bumped slightly as he returned to the tarmac. He shivered as a cold frisson enveloped him.

"Bloody hell! Sorry," Jack apologised, glancing at his passenger.

Flatcap's wife stared ahead into the darkness, oblivious. Jack looked back up the road at the disappearing tail lights. *Get it together.* He forced himself to refocus and follow them.

— 3 —

He had to survive. Jack had spent so many years alone, wishing for someone to share his life with. He didn't want to lose it all now. Thinking of surviving reminded him of the stories his nana had told him about living through World War Two. About how everyone had carried on as normal. How they looked after each other, helped one another when needed. How they'd sung songs down in the bomb shelters, frightened, scared, listening as the Luftwaffe rained down terror and misery. She would be telling Jack to "Keep calm and carry on."

Thinking about how his grandparents had survived the Blitz helped Jack to calm down. He reached out and turned on the stereo. Anything to try to distract him from the horror that he had just witnessed.

After thirty minutes, the two cars came up to an intersection. Flatcap pulled over, allowing Jack to pull alongside. His passenger jumped out before the car had stopped and ran over to her car. "Babies! Are you okay?" The kids clambered out of the car to hug her.

Jack waved to Flatcap. "You all right?"

"Yeah, I think so. Was that the virus?"

"I don't know, man. I really don't know." Jack shook

his head. "I was hoping you could tell me. I've been hiking in the mountains for the last three days."

"There was shaky footage on the news and conflicting reports," Flatcap said.

Jack nodded and checked his mirrors for any other cars.

So many thoughts were buzzing around in his head, he was having trouble concentrating. He just wanted to get home to Dee. A few hours ago he'd been happily enjoying the solitude of the wilderness, back before he read Dee's message. He'd believed her, but seeing the creatures first hand had frightened the hell out of him.

He looked back at Flatcap and his family. "We'd better keep moving."

Flatcap nodded in agreement. "Definitely. Which way from here?"

"Right for a few kilometres, then left for a bit. Just follow me. Lots of turns."

"Sure. How far to Cambridge?"

"Half an hour or so."

Flatcap grimaced and stuck his head out of his window and lowered his voice. "Thanks for your help back there."

"No problem."

Jack plotted the course in his head, thankful that his adventurous spirit had pushed him to explore all these back roads. The fact that he hated being stuck in traffic had added fuel to his passion for exploration. Everywhere he looked, the glow of fires in the direction of built-up areas lit up the night. Knowing what caused them made him hurry.

Coming over the brow of a hill, Jack saw the school

where he had to turn left. Realising he was going too fast, he pushed down on his brakes. Flatcap's car nudged into the back of his, causing him to spin, like in a police PIT manoeuvre. He wrenched the steering wheel hard left, trying to correct it, but Flatcap's car slammed into him again, causing both cars to slide out, tyres screeching. They ended up in the ditch on the side of the road.

Shaken, but unhurt, he clambered out of his car. His back wheels were stuck fast, deep down in the culvert. A short distance away, the other car's front end was also in the culvert.

Damn it. What else can go wrong tonight?

Jack made his way to Flatcap's car. "You guys all right?"

"Shaken but okay."

"We went crash!" squealed a child's voice. Jack smiled, spotting Flatcap's son in the back.

Flatcap hauled himself out of the car. "Yes son, we went crash."

He looked back at Jack. "What happened there?"

"Going too fast, simple as that. So do you think we can get these out?"

"Nah, I don't think so. We're in too deep."

"Bugger it!" Jack spat. "I'll go see if I can find a tractor or something. Plenty of farms around here."

Flatcap moved the peak of his hat up and down his brow. "Yeah, all right. Probably best I stay here with my family."

Jack nodded.

Returning to his car, he grabbed his pack out of the back seat, took out his headlamp and checked to see it was still working. Satisfied, he looked around. Spotting a driveway farther up the road, Jack headed off.

As he turned into the driveway, a crunch under his foot revealed gravel. Fear of being detected, by either humans or monsters, made him tread carefully and silently.

Jack flicked his gaze up towards the house and back to the vehicles. Plucking up his courage, he entered the property. As he crossed the cattle grate, his foot slipped and he went down, the resulting clang like a gunshot in the silence of the night. Jack winced, at the noise and the pain, and rubbed his foot. He prayed there were no monsters around to hear that racket. But surely they wouldn't be, so far from civilisation? He crawled off the cattle grate and got back onto his feet, testing out his foot. It would be fine. Dusting off his pants, he carried on up the driveway, pausing every few metres to strain his hearing for any sounds.

Jack could see the silhouettes of a house and vehicle sheds in the dark. Moving towards the shed, he thought he heard a popping sound. He froze. *What was that?* Heart hammering, he peered into the darkness. He wished he could turn on his light, but was fearful of attracting the creatures, or an angry farmer with a shotgun.

Maybe I should just knock on the door?

There were no lights on in the house, and no further sounds reached him. Jack wondered where everyone was. *Had they made a run for it? Why would they? They already lived in the country; nothing out here except cows, cows and more cows.* He shook these thoughts from his mind as he approached the shed.

The shed was enclosed on the sides and the back, leaving the front open to the elements; typical for farms.

He could see an old-looking tractor. Moving to the back of the vehicle, he saw that a wooden pallet platform was attached to the trailer. Piled on it was a rusty chain with a large metal hook attached to each end. In the cab, the key stuck out of the ignition.

Finally! Some good luck.

Jumping into the seat, he checked to see if the tractor was in neutral. With his fingers crossed, he turned the ignition.

The tractor coughed once, then turned over. Engaging the gear, Jack eased his way down the driveway. He looked back at the house every few seconds, half expecting someone or something to chase after him. But it all stayed quiet. He risked a quick glance up at the stars; he wished he and Dee were already in their cabin, doors bolted and safe. He sighed and focused on steering the old tractor.

Arriving back at the cars, he found Flatcap and his family sitting on the hood of their car, their feet resting against the small clay bank. The children were eating, nestled into their parents' sides.

"I'll reverse up and get yours first," Jack said, pointing at the front of the vehicle.

"All right," Flatcap nodded, pushing himself up.

"Don't chain it up around the axle. There should be a hook, near the front."

"Yup, sure thing."

Jack reached down and put the tractor in forward. Looking back up, he saw movement over Flatcap's shoulder.

Six figures were moving through the school yard. Their limbs seemed strange, elongated, their movements jerky, inhuman. Jack wasn't sure if they'd been spotted. But then one of the creatures let out a bloodcurdling scream. They all dropped to all fours and with an incredible burst of speed flew across the intervening ground towards the group.

Jack gave an inarticulate shout, but there was nothing he could do for Flatcap and his family. Within seconds, the monsters were on them. Two of the creatures slammed into Flatcap and his wife, tearing and snarling. The stench of blood permeated the air.

Time shifted into slow motion as Jack reacted. Thinking fast, he leaned over and grabbed the chain off the platform. Unfurling it, he swung it at the nearest creature, which had grabbed one of the boys. Slamming the hook into its head, he was shocked when bits of skull and black gooey sludge fountained out. The creature slumped against the car, dead.

Pulling the boy into the cab and onto his lap, Jack gunned the engine. The tractor lurched down the road. With one hand on the wheel, he swung the chain at two more of the creatures and searched for the second child. All he could see were the creatures fighting over what he guessed were the remains of Flatcap.

He swung the chain again at the snarling monsters. He couldn't believe how fast they were, easily dodging his wild swings.

The boy on his lap screamed in agony as one of the creatures tore open his leg. Jack managed to boot it in the face, smashing its sucker. It loosened its grip and Jack kicked it again, harder. He grinned as the beast fell off and crunched under the back wheels.

Three more of the creatures shrieked into the night

and sprinted towards the fleeing tractor, flanking them in a classic pincer movement.

Ugly, but not stupid.

Jack was still managing to keep one creature at bay with swings of his chain. He knew he couldn't outrun them on this old workhorse. He'd just have to outmanoeuvre them. The tractor might not have speed, but it did have torque.

Jack swung the wheel hard right, down a steep embankment.

Bounding over the rutted ground, the creatures drew closer.

So damn fast.

They slammed into the side of the tractor with abandon, causing it to tilt like a listing ship. Cradling the boy, and trying to tuck himself into a ball, he leapt off the vehicle. Thumping into the ground, the boy jolted free of Jack. Immediately, one the creatures caught up to the boy and, with a sickening sound, tore a hunk of muscle from his torso. The boy screamed, in terror and agony, his eyes finding Jack's. Pleading for the monster to stop. Pleading to not be left to die.

Jack rolled to a stop and found himself at the bottom of a ravine, next to a small bridge crossing over a river. Two blurs of black came flying towards him. To his surprise, he found he was still holding the chain. Channelling his inner Viking berserker, Jack swung the chain with all his remaining strength. It connected with the closest creature, smashing into its horror hole. It ripped away the monster's lower jaw and continued up through its eye socket, taking out black muck and brains and killing it instantly.

Before he could turn fully, the other creature careened into him, smashing him against the bridge railing. Pain streaked up his spine as his breath fled from his lungs.

The creature's sucker mouth snapped at him, its claws trying to grasp him. Jack swung his arms, fists clenched as he thumped a few blows against the beast. Kicking out, he fought with everything he had.

Jack managed to get the chain up under the monster's chin to hold off its snapping jaws, but the terrible stench of rotten fruit emanating from its mouth made him gag. One of its claws gouged deep into his thigh muscle. Jack let out a scream. He delved down deep inside himself and found an inner strength he never knew he had. He wrapped the chain around the creature's neck. Reaching behind him, he coiled it around the railing, then secured the hook over it. The creature dug its claws deeper into his thigh, its sucker mouth smacking at him as it strained to get at his face. With a last grunt of frustration, he tumbled over the railing, clasping the snapping creature in his arms. The chain went taut and, with his added weight, the creature's head ripped off, covering him in black gunk. Jack plunged towards the river, releasing the creature's body on the way down.

The cold water prickled his skin as he splashed into the water, its frigid embrace a welcome respite. He kicked back to the surface from the blackened depths. Gasping, Jack prepared himself to be torn apart by approaching reptilian nightmares.

To his surprise, the remaining creatures were still on the riverbank, apparently reluctant to enter the water. They snarled and hissed at him, joints popping as they paced up and down. He welcomed the reprieve.

Struggling to keep afloat, he removed his hiking pack and cradled it in his arms. Turning over, he let the current drag him away.

He stared up at the stars. His stars, the pinpricks of light.

Years of wondering what hellish creatures dwelled out in the infinite reaches of space, and Jack had never imagined he would find them on Earth.

I never knew their names...

I'm sorry, Dee...sorry...I tried...

— 4 —

Dee stared down at her smartphone, hoping for a signal. She paced the room, desperate to reach Jack again. But no matter where she held the phone, the bars remained empty. Sighing, she sat back down on the bed and pulled back the curtain. They lived in a two-storeyed house, with the garage and basement below. She was plagued by indecision, whether to hide down there or barricade herself upstairs. She got up again and walked around the room, her eyes flicking over their photos. Many were of them on various hikes around New Zealand. Others were of their travels around the world. She paused at the one of her, framed by a cascading waterfall. That was her favourite photo. It had been taken the day she met Jack.

"Dee, stop pacing. You're making me nervous."

She stopped and smiled faintly at Rachel, an old friend from school. They had recently reconnected. "Any word from Dion?"

"Nothing. I tried ringing the base too. No answer."

"I don't like it, Rach. You should come with us to the cabin. There's plenty of room."

"Thanks, Dee, but I can't. Dion said to wait at my parents'. He'll come to me."

"What was the last you heard?"

"All he said was that he was off to rescue some American official trapped on Tongariro."

"American?"

"Yup."

Dee mulled it over. Since media reports had told everyone to stay inside and lock their doors and that the army would come through their area, they had heard nothing. Not a peep.

Dee and Rachel sat in silence for another ten minutes. Dee listened to sounds outside, or lack of sound. An eerie silence had descended over the city. She and Jack lived on a busy street. It was all they could afford at the time, but she loved this house. Jack always commented that it had good bones. He had spent hours rewiring it to his standard, often coming home from his job as an electrician to strap on his work belt and crawl into the hot ceiling cavity. Dee would hear him muttering to himself about the bad workmanship done by others. She glanced up at the ceiling and wished he was up there now, muttering, not fifty kilometres away in the bush.

"I think I'll go, Dee," Rachel said, standing up and smoothing the creases in her jeans.

"Are you sure?"

"Yeah."

"At least let me drive you."

"Okay. That would be nice." Rachel flicked her eyes outside. "Do you think those things are here?"

"All we saw was that blurry video someone took in Auckland. Let's make it quick. Get home and lock your doors."

Rachel smiled and grabbed her handbag. She grasped

Dee's hand. "What about that policeman they found?"

"Who knows," Dee said. "I agree, though. It looked bad."

Rachel nodded and followed Dee outside.

The sun was sinking lower over the hills to the east as Dee edged her car out onto the normally busy road and turned left. As she drove down the road, she couldn't get over the lack of traffic. The lack of everything. It was if everyone had vanished. In a weird way, it reminded her of being in London in 1997. She was there on a working holiday when Princess Diana was killed in that car crash. The day of the funeral was eerie. London, one of the busiest cities in the world, became a ghost town. Dee and a friend had biked through the streets, a creepy feeling snapping at them. Dee glanced left and made the next turn. It felt exactly like that now. Hamilton, where she and Jack lived, was a tiny city, but on any other April day there was hustle and bustle as people went about their routines.

She sighed. "This is weird," she said, shaking her head. "Do your parents have any guns?"

"A few. Why?" Rachel said.

"I've got a strange feeling that we're going to need them."

"Huh," Rachel murmured.

Dee let the conversation go and drove on through the empty streets. Everywhere she looked, she saw cars parked on the road. Bikes abandoned. She even saw a golf cart parked outside someone's front door. Rachel's parents lived a few kilometres away, but thankfully not across the river. As she turned into Rachel's street, she slammed on the brakes. Standing in the street, his body rigid, was an old man in a dressing gown.

Dee looked at Rachel and shifted the car into neutral. "I'll go around."

"Wait," Rachel said, putting a hand on the dashboard.

The old man, now ten metres away, slowly turned around and stared at them. Blood was seeping out of his eyes and Dee could see dark patches all over his exposed skin.

"Eddie?" Rachel said. She made to leave the car but Dee grabbed her hand. "It's okay, Dee. He's my folks' neighbour."

Dee put her hand on the door handle. Something didn't feel right. Maybe Rachel was correct. Maybe the rumours about creatures attacking people were real. Maybe that shaky video was something real. Maybe. But she couldn't be sure.

Surely, with everyone having a camera at their disposal, they would have footage by now?

Dee chuckled to herself, remembering something Jack had said about UFOs.

You would think, with our technology, someone, somewhere would have decent footage.

She watched Rachel through the windscreen, that creeping feeling inching up her spine. Eddie turned at the sound of Rachel approaching and let out a weird shrieking sound. His eyes locked on her and he lunged, bringing her down.

Dee gasped and bolted out of the car. Rachel was struggling to hold off the old man. He had her pinned down with his knees and was trying to bite her throat.

Dee dropped her shoulder and thumped into Eddie, knocking him off Rachel. Eddie rolled once and leapt into a crouch. The speed of his movements amazed Dee. Eddie snarled and let out another weird shriek. This time, other shrieks answered. Dee glanced at Rachel. Her eyes were wide and she clutched at her handbag, kneading it like it was a lump of dough.

Dee grasped her hand and pulled her back towards the car, all the time keeping an eye on Eddie. He watched them move but made no indication that he was going to charge again. Instead, saliva drooled from the corners of his mouth. That was when Dee noticed his mouth had shrivelled and his lips had turned black.

"Rachel," Dee whispered, "when I say, run to the car and lock your door."

"Yup."

"Now!" Dee cried. She let go of Rachel's hand and pivoted. Straining, she leapt for her open door. A piercing howl jolted her head up.

Three more figures were sprinting down the road towards them. Rachel let out a scream as Eddie caught her and tackled her to the ground for a second time.

Dee skidded to a stop and changed direction as Rachel disappeared under him. He seemed stronger and more agile now.

"Get off!" she screamed, kicking and punching.

Frantic, Dee searched for a weapon, anything, but came up short. More shrieks filled the air, reminding her of the new threat. She paused. Conflicted, Dee didn't know what to do. Help Rachel and risk both of them dying, or flee?

She grimaced and slammed into Eddie with her shoulder. There was no way she was going to let her friend down. Eddie rocked back but held on. His movement pushed Dee off balance and she tumbled to the ground, sprawling on the pavement.

Her skin tore on the concrete. Dee winced and shook her head. Rachel had used the distraction to kick Eddie the rest of the way off her. She hoisted Dee to her feet.

The others were only twenty metres away now, their shrieks filling the air with a bone-chilling din.

Dee yanked Rachel's hand. "Run!"

Dee spotted their destination halfway down the road. She pumped her legs, thankful to Jack for the many hours of hiking up hills. The exercise had conditioned her muscles. She ran faster, hoping Rachel was still behind her.

The thing about being chased is that you enter a surreal state, like an ancient genetic memory that boils up to the surface and forces its way into your mind. Your brain screams, "Flee!" over and over. Adrenaline floods your body, giving muscles new energy.

Dee risked a peek over her shoulder. Half to check on her friend and half to see the location of the creatures that pursued them. Dee shook her head. She was having a hard time comprehending what was happening. So the rumours were true. The virus did something to you. Mutated you into something primeval. Whatever it did, all Dee could think of was "Run!"

Rachel sprinted past her in a burst of speed as they reached her parents' house. As she made up the last few metres, she fumbled for her keys in her handbag.

"Hurry!" Dee said. She reached Rachel and spun around. The creatures were coming up fast.

"I can't find the keys!" Rachel screamed, her voice coming out in a high-pitched squeal. She banged her fist against the door, shouting. But the house remained quiet.

Dee picked up the rubbish bin next to the front step and hurled it at the nearest creature. Its yellow eyes flared back at her. The rubbish bin bounced off its head. It had been a man once. Now his skin had a translucent glow to it, showing veins and arteries. He was mostly bald, but she could still see tufts of hair. The man stumbled and tripped over, sprawling on the ground.

"Go!" Dee shouted, cursing to herself. They needed weapons, and fast. They darted down the side of the house and through the wooden side gate, locking it behind them. Immediately the beasts chasing them slammed into the timber. It creaked and wobbled, but held.

"What do we do, Dee?" Rachel whispered.

"We need to hide or find something to fight with, fast."

"Dad has some tools in his shed," Rachel said. She gestured at the glasshouse and tin shed in the corner of the section. Large, well-maintained gardens led up to the door.

"That'll have to do. C'mon," Dee said.

Dee cast her eyes over the peg board that lined the back wall of the shed. Rachel's father had every tool she could think of. Garden forks, spades. Dutch hoe. Weird tilling implements. She smiled when she spotted an axe leaning against the bench. Rachel grabbed a machete and hefted it, checking its weight.

Thumps and shrieks echoed around the back yard. Dee felt a little better with something to fight back with. She took a couple of seconds to refocus and pictured her car a couple of hundred metres down the road. She pictured them running to it, getting into it and getting the hell out of here.

"Are you ready?" Dee asked, looking at her friend.

Rachel grimaced, and sighed. "Yeah."

"We're going to run out the other gate and get to my car, all right?"

"Okay."

Dee grasped Rachel's shoulder. "We have to do it. Okay?"

"Yeah. I'm just scared, Dee. I'm not used to this sort of thing."

Dee smiled. A soft smile. She knew what Rachel meant. For so long, many humans had lived lives of luxury. Lives that kings from the Middle Ages could only have dreamed of. Medicine. Food. Technology. Flushing toilets. Roads. Everything.

"No one is. But I want to live. To see Jack again. I'm not becoming food for whatever those creatures are."

Several sounds reached Dee. The gate rattled and splintered. A howl rang out, answered by several shrieks. She ducked below the bench and looked over into the adjacent glasshouse, hoping for somewhere to hide.

Dee spotted a pile of compost and, next to it, potting mix. She crawled over and began to dig as more howls filled the air.

Rachel soon joined her at the task. Within a few seconds, they had made a large enough indent. Dee grabbed some bamboo stakes and shovelled the compost over her legs and torso. The soil caved in, burying them underneath. Dee pushed the bamboo stake out and tested it for air. She couldn't see her friend in the dark, but she could feel her shaking. Dee shut her eyes and hoped they had done enough.

— 5 —

The chill of the water surprised Jack. It seeped through his soft tissue and into his bones. He could feel his body shaking, trying to warm itself up. If he wasn't careful, he'd get hypothermia.

He hugged his pack closer to his chest and looked around. The creatures were still following him, their strange yellow eyes watching his every move. They howled and shrieked as they scampered along the banks. Occasionally the trees became too thick for them to follow but Jack could hear them just out of sight. Sometimes a creature would sniff the air and tear off, away from the river, a few of them following after. They could be gone for twenty minutes, sometimes half an hour, but, like terminators, they came back to track him relentlessly in his course down the river.

As Jack floated, he pondered what he knew about the creatures so far. If he was being honest, very little. They were fast. They attacked in a frenzied pack, like land piranhas. Jack barked out a laugh, thinking of a horror movie with flying piranhas he had once watched with his brother.

At least these beasts can't fly.

He shook his head. He could just picture Dee telling him off for daydreaming about movies and not concentrating on the task ahead of him.

Jack shivered and glanced around. What he needed was a log, anything, to float on, and fast. The banks were clear of the monsters right now as they had run off howling a few minutes earlier, having picked up some scent or other. Jack let out a breath and swam for shore. He aimed for a copse of willow trees and hauled himself out of the river. Water cascaded off his chilled, exhausted body. He picked out a suitable tree for a flotation device and shuffled along the trunk. It was a small tree but it held his weight.

He strained his ears for any sounds of the creatures returning, but their shrieks were coming from some distance away. Not wanting to waste any more time, Jack opened his pack and took out his emergency dry-bag. He had a spare change of clothes, some rations and a first-aid kit inside. As fast as he could, he pulled off his wet clothes and towelled himself dry.

Having on dry clothes warmed him and gave him new determination to make it home. Home to Dee. Home meant everything to Jack. It was his haven, and Dee was the rock at its centre.

He contemplated what to do next. He knew he had to get back into the river. It was the only option. But getting wet again wasn't. He bounced on the tree, testing the strength of the timber. He had a small, collapsible saw in his pack.

Working quickly, Jack set about his task. When he'd managed to saw through half of the log, he jumped down onto the muddy bank to finish the job. Feverish in his fear of the creatures' return, he sped up. Tiny wood chips and sawdust coated his shoes. Just as the log began to splinter, he heard howls and crashes nearby. He pricked his ears, trying to determine which direction they were coming from.

Just a little more time.

Five centimetres to go. More shrieks. Branches shattered around him. The beasts could smell him. Jack glanced around. Through the willows, he could see the glowing yellow eyes of one of the creatures just a few metres away. It was sniffing the air. As he watched, its deformed head kissed the ground, then jolted back up.

Three centimetres to go.

"Help!" A frantic scream tore through the night.

Jack paused from his sawing and looked behind him. Had he really heard that?

"Please! Someone!" it screamed again, closer this time.

"Over here," Jack called out. There was no use trying to hide his position; the creatures knew where he was. Jack had gambled that they wouldn't reach him in time.

At last the log snapped with a crash and splashed down in the shallow water. The creature a few metres away howled and bounded towards Jack. In seconds, it had reached him and slammed onto the log. Jack threw his pack onto his makeshift raft and pushed the log into deeper water, ignoring the beast for now. He straddled the log like it was a surfboard and scanned for the source of the frantic cries.

"Wait!" shouted the voice.

Jack twisted and gawked as a woman broke through the thick trees and waded into the river. She held out a hand, pleading, towards Jack, her eyes wide in fear. She had twigs and mud tangled in her thick mane of hair.

"Swim. Hurry," Jack said. He looked at the beast perched on the end of his raft. It was staring at the water as if some innate sense told it not to enter. To stay out. Danger.

The woman dived into the water and managed to reach the log. Jack didn't watch her; he was too busy keeping an eye on the creature. It was crouching dead-still, only moving its eyes. The makeshift raft rocked as the woman pulled herself half out of the river.

Howls and shrieks erupted from the banks in a cacophony of noise. The monsters had returned en masse. Hearing his brethren screeching stirred something in their passenger. It snapped its head up and glared at Jack. Its eyes flicked to the woman. She screamed and dropped back into the river. With a shriek, the monster bounded at Jack. He fell back and jabbed the saw into the beast's throat. The jagged blade pierced the creature's neck and went up into its sucker mouth. Jack grunted and tried to shove the monster off. It clasped Jack and thrashed about. Jack slammed the palm of his hand against the saw's handle, embedding it deeper into the creature's mouth. He hit the handle again. The creature let out an almost pitiful whimper and went still. Disgusted at the thick black blood that oozed over his arm, Jack kicked the beast into the water.

The creatures that lined the river shrieked at the smell of blood, whether his or the beast's, Jack had no idea. He reached out and helped the woman from the water. She clung to the tree, gasping, as they floated away. Jack left her to catch her breath and turned around, watching the dark countryside slowly drift by. He had a rough idea where they were. The river seemed to be taking them west, towards the Waikato River and Lake Arapuni. He hoped he was right. If he could find a kayak or, better still, a motorboat, he could stay on the Waikato all the way to Hamilton. To Dee.

"Thank you," the woman gasped. She was still lying on the log, clutching a branch. Jack could see her jeans and shirt had been torn in several places. She had dozens of bleeding scratches and a deep wound on her arm.

"No worries," Jack said. He nodded towards her myriad cuts. "You okay?"

"Barely," she said, moving slightly to face him. "They nearly got me back there."

"What happened?"

"You first. I still need to catch my breath."

Jack opened his pack and handed her his spare water bottle. She took it and gulped it down.

"I'm Jack."

"Emma."

He let her keep the water and offered her a protein bar. He wanted to keep them for himself, not knowing how long it would take him to get home, but the good side of him wanted to help.

Emma looked up at him. "So, what happened to you?"

Jack sighed and relayed all that had happened to him in the ten hours since receiving the news. Emma listened, nodding, but offered no questions. Finally, Jack was finished.

"Hamilton, eh?" Emma said, chewing on the last of the bar.

"Yeah. Long way to go. Especially with those things out there," Jack grumbled. "They seem to be afraid of the water, so I'm going to hunt for a boat."

"Good idea. Mind if I tag along?" Emma murmured. "What about going to an evac centre on the way?"

"Evac centre?"

"Last announcement I heard on the radio, it told everyone to head to the nearest evacuation site. Cambridge would be our closest."

"We could check it out on the way. But my main concern is getting home to Dee," Jack said. "What about your family?"

Emma turned away and gazed over the farmland. She leant back against a branch and rubbed at the congealed blood on her arm. She examined Jack before letting out a sigh. "He came back, you know."

"Who?"

"My husband." Emma pointed back to where they had met. "We have a small dairy farm. A few sheep. Living away from town, we were used to having plenty of food. We figured we would just wait it out. Yesterday, we heard screams. Jon went to help. After a few hours, I started to freak out. Jon had shown me, years ago, how to use the shotgun. As I was fetching it, he came home." Emma paused, and turned her head away. When she turned it back, Jack could see the tears glistening in the early morning light. "I knew something was different as soon as I heard to the screen door bang open. I don't know if it was the weight of his feet on the floor or just the way he was standing. Whatever it was, he attacked me."

Jack waited, but Emma stayed silent. He didn't press her. They had both done things to survive. Things Jack had never really imagined himself doing in a million years. He swivelled around and faced forwards. The creatures still tracked them downstream.

The sun was slowly rising over the Kaimai mountains. Jack watched as the sky went from grey to pink. Orange to yellow, and finally blue. He shifted his gaze north and prayed that Dee was safe.

— 6 —

They were scratching around out there, clawing at the ground. Dee could hear them sniffing. She could even hear their breath rattling out of their lungs as though they all had a bad infection. She alternated between sucking air through her makeshift snorkel and holding her breath. Somehow, the compost had the creatures confused. They seemed to know that she and Rachel were in here somewhere but couldn't figure out where.

Dee kept herself still and focused on taking small, shallow breaths. She recalled the calming technique Jack had taught her and used it now to remain still. Dee could feel Rachel next to her. She would move her hand an inch or two now and then, but otherwise stayed as motionless as Dee.

The creatures sniffed around for several more minutes, scratched at the floor and let out the occasional shriek.

Finally, she heard them leave the shed and felt the vibrations of their strange, contorted limbs as they thumped across the yard. Rachel began to move but Dee held her back with a gentle hand on an arm, still fearful of the beasts. They could have left a sentry behind. It could all be a trick to lull them into a trap.

Without a visual, Dee wasn't going to move unless she was certain. She counted to one hundred, then slowly dug away at the smelly compost and scraped some egg shells and vegetable scraps off her. She looked around.

It was now fully dark. The shed was empty, but Dee could see several footprints in the dry potting mix. She waited a few more minutes before digging the rest of her way out. Rachel rolled out of the soil and picked some celery leaves out of her hair.

"Eww," she whispered.

"Look for your keys, Rach. We'll hide inside."

Rachel pulled the keys free and jangled them.

Dee held her finger to her lips, shushing her. "Not so loud. Okay?"

"I only have a key for the front door," Rachel said. "I hope Mum and Dad are okay."

"I hope so too, Rach," Dee said.

Dee crept forwards, clutching the axe tightly, and scanned the back yard. It too was free of the creatures. Faint howls could be heard in the distance, but nothing came from close by. She pointed towards the front door and nodded at Rachel.

Dee inched her way down the side of the house, keeping her left shoulder hard up against the bricks, axe held ready. A faint odour of rotting fruit hung in the air. Dee sniffed, trying to pinpoint it, but couldn't determine if it was just the compost or something else.

They reached the front of the house without seeing any of the creatures. Dee's abandoned car was visible halfway down the street.

So close. But so far.

Rachel moved up beside her. "I can't see any of those

things," she whispered.

"I don't like it. It's too quiet."

"I just want to get out of here and inside."

"Okay. On three."

"Yup."

"One." Dee glanced left. Clear.

"Two." She looked right. Clear.

"Three."

Dee pushed off the wall and slid the axe into her right hand. Rachel screamed, Dee pivoted and gasped. The creature was on top of her friend, latched onto her back and tearing at her head and neck. Rachel screamed again and rolled to one side, trying to dislodge the beast.

The beast turned and its yellow reptile-like eyes bored into Dee's. Its lips curled back into a snarl and it snapped its jaws at her friend.

A shriek from above jolted Dee from her stupor. Another creature leapt down from the roof and landed next to the first. It met Dee's eyes. Even in the dark, she could see a glow coming from them, which invoked a fear within her that she never knew she had. This was something new. Something evil. The beast in front of her thought of her as food. Nothing more. Nothing less. And it was going to do everything it could to get that food. Her.

The beast had once been a woman, a half-torn skirt still in evidence around its waist. What had been blouse was now ripped and tattered, leaving the lace bra underneath visible. It hung loose on the shrivelled skin.

The creature crouched down and snarled at Dee before leaping at her.

For the thousandth time in the last few hours, Dee

wished she had a gun or even her katana. She swung the axe with everything she had. Every last bit of strength. She not only swung it for her survival, but out of pity. Pity for the woman the creature had been.

The axe caught the monster in the side of the head and ripped off its lower jaw. Dark blood arced out over the lawn. The beast rolled over and righted itself.

Dee risked a quick peek at her friend. The creature had slammed her onto her front and was tearing at her back and head. Rachel was fighting, but failing fast, her shouts now coming in short, anguished cries.

Dee turned her attention back to the beast in front of her. She had to end this, and fast. Growling, she charged the monster. It gurgled something and swung its hands at Dee as she ducked beneath its groping limbs and drove the axe into the beast's chest. It sank deep, shattering ribs and tearing away flesh.

A putrid rotten fruit scent invaded her nose. Dee shook her head and kicked the monster to the ground. It was still alive and tried to stand.

"Sorry," Dee murmured. She swung the axe again, this time silencing the poor creature.

Dee spun and searched out Rachel. Rachel had her hand outstretched, begging for help. Begging for mercy. The creature that had once been a man was tearing strips of flesh from her neck.

Dee cried out and drove the blade of the axe deep into the creature's head. It gurgled blood and slumped over, the axe still buried deep.

Dee glanced left and right, praying that no other monsters were coming. Several of the creatures appeared by her car and, spotting her, began to run.

"Get up, Rach," Dee said, tugging on Rachel's hand. When Rachel didn't move, she frowned and crouched down. "Rach?"

She was staring blankly up at Dee, her lips moving in a whisper. Dee crouched down and grasped her hand. "Tell Dion I love him…I…sorry…" Blood and saliva bubbled from her lips.

"You tell him. Get up. We can make it," Dee said, glancing towards her car. The beasts were only a hundred metres away but closing fast.

Dee slammed her fist on the ground in frustration. She didn't want to leave her friend to become these creatures' next meal, but she knew she was no good to anyone dead. With a growl, she shouted out a curse to the creatures and ran. Ran with everything she had.

Houses flew by in a blur. She jumped over kids' toys, gardens and bikes. As she sprinted, Dee wondered where all the bodies or remains were. If these beasts were eating everyone, where were the remains?

She risked a quick peek over her shoulder. She had managed to lose three of the monsters but some, maybe four, still chased her.

Dee spotted a mountain bike lying in the middle of the road. A dark stain had spread out around it. Trying not think about exactly what the stain was, Dee skidded to a stop and snagged the bike.

Anything beats running.

Frantic, Dee searched for an escape route. She and Jack had spent many afternoons cycling through the city, exploring its many bike paths.

A lone howl echoed down the street, chilling Dee. She knew she had to decide, and fast. She looked down the road and grinned when she spotted a sign for the river. With one last glance to her pursuers, she pedalled away down the steep hill that led to the river path.

Dee breathed out a sigh of relief as the path ahead remained clear of creatures, and behind her, their howls wailed in the breeze.

Images of Rachel dying in a pool of blood, her arm outstretched in a plea for help, motivated her onwards into the night.

— 7 —

The province of Waikato is a mixture of low-lying swamps, riverlands and hundreds of farms. Filled with ravines and gullies, it is surrounded by mountains: the Kaimais to the east, the Hikramatas to the north, and Pirongia and Maungatautari to the west and south. Dissecting the province in half is New Zealand's longest river, also named the Waikato. Several hydroelectric power stations were built to meet the demand for electricity. As a result, man-made lakes like Karapiro and Arapuni dominate the landscape.

Jack basked in the sun, enjoying the warmth of the late morning as the log drifted across Lake Arapuni. He could hear the creatures howling on the shore but didn't bother to look. They were always going to be there, waiting for him and Emma to make a mistake. He glanced at Emma. She was hugging the main branch, her chest rising and falling at a steady rate. Jack envied her for being able to sleep, on a log, in the middle of a big river, with killer monsters on its banks. He had managed to catch a few minutes here and there, but worry, as always, plagued his mind.

What if the log drifts to shore?

What if I fall asleep and drown?
What if we get sucked into the intake pipe?
What if... What if...

He groaned to himself and took another sip of water. During the early morning he had refilled the water bladder from the lake, dropping in a couple of purifying tablets just to be sure. He shivered with revulsion, just thinking about getting sick from giardia, the pesky parasite found in fresh water.

Emma jumped, clung to the log and opened one eye. She scrubbed at her face with a hand. "I was having a horrible nightmare."

"Morning."

"I dreamt that a virus had made everyone sick, and now monsters chased us." Emma turned her head.

Jack grinned as she looked at the creatures running along the distant shore. He frowned, noticing that their numbers had dropped significantly.

"Oh wait. It's not a dream," Emma said. Her mouth twitched into a sardonic grin.

"Are you always so cheerful in the morning?" Jack asked. "Especially in these circumstances?"

"Shush, Grumpy," Emma groaned, splashing water on her face. "Besides, it could be worse."

"Worse?"

"Could have been shot." She laughed. "And at least we're outside."

Jack's tired mind twigged to her reference. "Always look on the bright side, huh?"

"That's the spirit," Emma said. "Now, what's for breakfast?"

"I've got some food in my pack. Help me paddle to

that pontoon first." He gestured to a small platform about five hundred metres from the lake shore. Directly beyond it was a campground.

With both of them using their hands to paddle, they made short work of reaching the pontoon. Now that he was closer, Jack could make out its construction: it was simply six forty-four-gallon drums lashed together with wooden planking secured on top to make a square platform. Jack could just picture children swimming out to it and using it to dive into the lake, making as big a splash as possible. He tried to recall what the pastime was called but couldn't remember. Something like "manus".

Jack combed through his bright green hiking pack. He kept an emergency box of rations in the bottom. He liked to keep a six-pack of MREs along with protein bars and, of course, chocolate.

He offered an MRE to Emma. "Chicken and noodle. Fresh off the stove."

"What is that?" Emma said, frowning at the purple and white packaging.

"MRE," Jack said. "Meals. Ready to Eat."

Emma raised an eyebrow but accepted the food.

"Look. You can heat it," Jack said. He spent a minute showing her how to heat the food before doing his own. They floated silently on the pontoon, enjoying the high calorie meal and the light of the sun. Relaxing on the spacious pontoon after the painful excursion on the narrow log that had been their saviour for the last six hours.

Jack kept an eye on the creatures and noted their numbers dwindling as the sun grew in strength. April was his favourite time of year as the last of the summer heat hung around, keeping the days warm though the nights were cool.

"Waiter. I'm ready for my dessert now," Emma said.

"Chocolate?"

"You have chocolate?" Emma grinned. "And you gave me that MRE? What did you call it again?"

"Meals. Ready to Eat."

"More like 'Meals. Regurgitate till empty'." Emma groaned, holding her stomach.

Jack barked out a laugh. "I've heard them called 'Meals. Requiring enemas'." He winked.

"I'll say. Oh well. Beggars can't be choosers. Now cough up, Townie."

Jack smiled as he handed her a Whittaker's peanut slab. He still had a small stash in another compartment, so was confident of it lasting until he reached Dee. Thinking of Dee, Jack cast his eyes north, past the towering bush-covered mountain of Maungatautari to its sister peak, Pirongia. He could just make out the top third and smiled wistfully.

Hold on, Dee.

"You don't happen to have a first-aid kit in that box of tricks, do you?" Emma asked.

"Sure do."

He looked down at the wound in his leg as he handed her the kit. Jack was surprised that he hadn't thought of it since last night. It still throbbed and, inspecting it, he could see that blood had congealed around the torn flesh. It would definitely need some professional attention, and the sooner the better.

Jack set about field-dressing the wound. He swapped items with Emma as she cleaned out the dozens of scratches on her arms and legs. After he'd wrapped a thick bandage around his leg, he spent some time checking that he had no other injuries.

"Can you do the cuts on my back?" Emma said, handing him the tube of disinfectant.

"Okay."

As they worked, Jack continued to watch the shore. At some point, all the creatures vanished. He strained his ears, listening out for their terrifying howls, but the wilderness remained silent.

"What do you think?" Jack said. "Make a run for it?"

"Yeah. I need to attend to this wound better. Get some stitches." Emma held up her wrist. "Where are we exactly?"

"I think the town of Arapuni is a little way down that road."

Emma nodded. "I can't see any of those things, so I say let's go."

Together they propelled the log to a sandy beach that had a concrete boat ramp at one end. Jack patted the log as he shrugged into his pack. It was strange how you could get attached to inanimate objects. The willow log had kept them safe when they'd needed it most. He looked around, scanning his immediate vicinity. Jack knew he needed a weapon. Anything that would give him a better chance at survival. A better chance to see his wife again.

Spotting the campground maintenance shed, he tapped Emma on the shoulder, pointed and took off at a steady jog. He heard her fall in step behind him.

The roller door was up, bathing the shed in natural light. The heavy stench of petrol, oil and cut grass hung in the air. A red ride-on lawnmower lay abandoned on its side, its blades lying haphazardly next to it. Tools were scattered about, as though whoever had been working on the machine had left in a hurry. Jack let his eyes wander over the rest of the workshop. He spotted hammers and chisels. Spanners. Wrenches. Lots of mechanical tools but nothing he was happy using for a weapon. Emma brushed past him and grabbed a jacket off a hook. She turned it over before slipping into it.

Jack walked through the shed but came up weaponless. He went to the door of a smaller room that joined onto the garage and spied exactly what he wanted. Something with a blade. A bachi hoe. It was similar to a pickaxe but had only one wedge-shaped blade, primarily used for digging out weeds or harvesting.

Jack tested its weight, turning it over in his hand. He felt better having something to defend himself against the beasts.

Emma picked up an axe and turned to face him. "I'm a lumberjack, okay?"

Jack shook his head and smiled. "Let's go." He pushed past her to stand in the doorway.

"What? No sing-song?"

Jack stopped in his tracks and forced out a breath. Normally he would play along and goof around, but all he wanted was to get back to Dee. He had wasted too much time as it was. Way too much time. "I just want to get home to my wife, okay. So I'm sorry if I don't join with you in singing the lumberjack song." Jack pointed outside with his bachi hoe. "Those monsters could come back any second. We need to get around the dam, find a boat and get back on the water. All before getting torn apart."

Emma held up her hands in mock surrender. "Okay." She looked down at the floor and murmured something Jack couldn't hear.

"I'm sorry, Emma. I'm just really tired. Worried, and, to be honest, freaked out by what's going on."

"I know, Jack. I am too," Emma said, grinning. "Serious face from now on."

Jack grimaced and took a few seconds to refocus. He had always had a short temper. For years he had struggled with keeping it in check. Meditation and not drinking coffee helped, but the stress of the last twenty-four hours weighed heavily on his mind.

"No problem. Let's just go," Jack sighed.

Emma led them out of the campground and down the main road of Arapuni. It was a small rural town with only one shop, a dairy, a small convenience-type store, the windows of which lay broken all over the car park. The shelves had been ransacked. Even so, Jack stopped to look and found a few bars of chocolate and some water. The cash register had been smashed open and all the money taken.

Jack shook his head at the destruction. He bet that if he checked, all the tobacco would be gone. It was weird what people took over what they really needed.

They travelled on in silence. Jack searched the left side of the road and Emma took care of the right. The houses here were a mixture of brick and wood. Some were well maintained, while others needed some TLC. There were plenty of vehicles but no boats. On they walked through the small town and out down an empty country road beyond. Jack wanted to try his luck down by Lake Karapiro with its mansions and large farms. Surely one of them had a motorboat?

Emma nudged his side and gestured. Just up ahead was a gated community with a black metal gate framed by two gatehouses.

Jack inched his way forwards and peered in through the gatehouse window. Seeing nothing, he reached through the half window and pressed the green button. The whir of the gate opening brought a smile to his lips. He made eye contact with Emma and followed her through.

Jack gazed into the sky, noting that the sun was dropping slowly to the west. He hoped that the creatures would give them a little more time.

Emma grasped his arm and smiled. Sitting in the driveway of a massive house was a speed boat, sleek, white and shiny, begging to be used. Jack scanned around, hunting for a vehicle, anything that could be used to tow the boat. He peeked in the garage window and grinned.

Sitting inside was a 4x4.

Maybe, just maybe, their luck was changing.

— 8 —

Dee shuddered every time she heard a scream. When she first made it to the river path, all was quiet as she cycled along. But the deeper she got into the city and the closer she got to their house, the more frequent the screams became. Dee stopped her bike near the golf course and crouched down behind some bushes. She had spotted dark figures running across the greens, heading in her direction. After what had happened with Rachel and the creatures that prowled that neighbourhood, she was being cautious.

As the figures drew nearer, Dee could see they were the size of children. She watched their gaits carefully, trying to gauge if they were humans or creatures. The creatures had a strange way of walking, as if their spines had been bent, and they turned their heads constantly.

Dee observed them for a few more moments. Finally, convinced these children were not creatures, she decided she was safe. Standing, she let out a whistle, trying to get their attention. Now that they were closer, she counted five kids. Two were taller, while the other three appeared to be primary school-age. They came to a stop a few metres away. The taller kids were armed with a broomstick and a machete respectively.

Machete held his weapon up, showing Dee he was armed.

"Hey," Dee said, holding up her hands.

"What do you want?" Machete answered, his voice and manner gruff.

"I just want to make sure you're okay."

"We don't need your help, lady," Machete said. He waved it around again. "We can look after ourselves."

Dee nodded and cast her eyes over the smaller children. They clutched each other and stared at her with wide eyes, their sclera shining in the bright moonlight. "Where are your parents?"

Machete nudged Broomstick and chortled. "You're well munted, ain't you?" He pointed back past the golf course. "Everyone is dead, girl. Or become one of those things." He stared at Dee, holding his machete across his chest.

"Why don't you come back to my house. We can wait for my husband to get back and then we'll get out of the city."

"Nah. We're heading to the posh school across the river. Plenty of food, and we can lock it up good."

"I don't think that's a good idea. What do you think you're going to do with a machete and a broomstick against those things?" Dee asked. "We need the army, or guns."

Machete scoffed and pulled Broomstick's arm. "C'mon, let's go."

They both turned and walked away, ending the conversation. Dee watched them go, torn. She wanted to make sure they were safe, but from the way the smaller children followed the two teenagers, it was obvious that they either knew each other or were a family. A couple of the smaller children looked back as they disappeared into the trees that lined the path.

Sighing, Dee mounted her borrowed bike and pressed on. She thanked Jack silently for his insistence on exploring. They had spent many summer days cycling around the river and along Hamilton's many bike paths. He'd shown her how they linked into gullies and onto main roads. Dee pictured the route ahead, mapping it out. Judging it by population density. She calculated the risk and figured that it didn't matter. Sometimes you could plan something to death and a little quirk, some little incident of chance, turned it to chaos.

Dee slowed to take a sharp bend when a scream pealed through the night, followed by shouts and high-pitched squeals. The squeals sounded like children. *The children!* Dee slammed on the brakes. The screams had come from the direction Machete had taken with the kids. Cursing herself for letting them go, Dee swung her bike around and pushed down hard on the pedals.

The wind whistled in her ears as she raced back down the path, the screams and squeals continuing to guide her. She rounded another bend and skidded to a stop. Three of the creatures had Machete and Broomstick pinned against a tree. Broomstick thrust his weapon at one of the beasts, but it was like poking at a tiger with a straw. The creature snarled and swatted away the stick. The monster still had on a flannel shirt, though it was torn and hanging in shreds.

Dee didn't pause to think, she reacted purely on instinct. Seeing the creatures hunting the children stirred something deep inside her. A motherly impulse boiled up and burst out.

Dee lifted the bike above her head and smashed it down onto the creature snarling at Broomstick. As the bike connected with its head, it grunted and slumped to the ground. Dee shifted her grip and shoved the bike on top of the middle beast. It shrieked and screeched, clawing at the metal frame.

Machete used the distraction and hacked at the creature in front of him. The blade dug deep into its shoulder. The beast snarled and leapt onto Machete. In a flash it had wrapped its claw-like hands around his neck and latched on. Machete screamed as the creature tore off a chunk his flesh and ripped out his throat. Blood arced out over Dee as she kicked out at the beast under her bike. With a sudden burst of strength, it kicked her to the ground and threw the bike into the bushes.

Dee sat up, gasping for breath. The force of the creature's throw had knocked the wind from her lungs. Her eyes flicked around, searching for a weapon. Broomstick was leaning against the tree, a hand holding his stomach. Blood seeped through his fingers.

The beast clawed at the ground like a bull and howled into the night sky. Myriad howls answered it. Dee was stunned by the number. A few hours ago these beasts had been just a rumour, just grainy footage on the news. Now they were a nightmarish reality.

"Throw me the broom!" Dee cried out, her hand outstretched. She jumped to her feet and caught the broomstick. Immediately she snapped it over her knee, and just in time. The creature lunged at her.

Dee thrust her makeshift spear into its chest and it fell

backwards, landing with a thump. The broomstick carried on through the deformed beast. It howled in agony and snapped its weird mouth at Dee.

Bringing her legs up, she used her thighs to hug the creature and hunted for the other broken half of the broom. Howls reverberated from the direction of the golf course, joining the cacophony of sounds that pounded her head. Dee was having trouble focussing. More and more howls drew closer. She needed to end this, and fast.

"Help me!" she called out to Broomstick. She heard a grunt and felt a thud on the ground. Broomstick had collapsed. He was struggling to hold out the other end of the broken stick, his fingers coated in his own blood.

Dee let out a scream of frustration, grasped the stick firmly and drove it into the skull of the beast, finally silencing it. She pushed it away and clambered groggily to her feet, a stick in each hand.

The creature feeding on Machete was ignoring her, so engrossed in its meal it didn't sense Dee as she jogged up behind it and drove a stick through its head. It gurgled once and fell down next to the dead teenager. Dee glimpsed the mess it had made of Machete and stumbled back, bile rising in her throat. She clenched her teeth and swallowed.

Pivoting, she searched behind her for the sources of the howls she had heard. Dark smudges moved across the greens of the golf course, confirming they were still on her trail. Looking for food. Hunting.

The creature she had knocked unconscious stirred and rolled over. Dee chastised herself for not finishing it off.

Rule #2: Double tap.

She grunted and drove the other broken stick through

its skull. It sank in as if the creature's skull was made of clay.

"Lady. Up here," a small voice whispered.

Dee glanced up and blinked rapidly. Machete and Broomstick had been stupid thinking they could hide out in the school, but they had been brave in their instinct to sacrifice themselves to protect the children.

"Jump down. Hurry," Dee said.

The child shook his head and pointed behind her. "They're coming."

Reaching down, Dee extracted the blood-covered machete from the dead creature and hauled herself up the tree. Like many of the trees lining the river, it was a weeping willow and had thick branches that draped down over the water. Dee eyed the fast-flowing Waikato River and weighed up her options. If it came down to it, she would dive in with the kids and float downstream. Anything to get away from the claws and teeth of the beasts.

The shrieks of the monsters grew louder as they drew closer. A whole pack was now moving across the greens. Dee noted how they paused and sniffed the air before moving again. If a new beast joined the pack, the others would smell it, shriek at each other and move on.

As she huddled in the tree with the children, several creatures broke away from the pack and sprinted towards them. She guessed the blood of Machete and Broomstick was like candy to them, like the smell of baking bread to humans.

Within seconds they were at the tree, and without hesitation they crouched down over the bodies and went into a feeding frenzy. The children beside her whimpered.

Dee raised her finger to her lips, urging them to remain silent. All she could hope for was that the monsters would be too caught up in their meals to notice the feast above them.

A dozen more creatures crested the hill, howling. The feeding creatures paused their grisly meal to shriek at the new arrivals. There was a brief second of silence before the new creatures charged. They joined the beasts below them and fought over the scraps. Dee hugged the tree tight, mesmerised by the horror of the scene unfolding below. One creature broke away, clutching a leg. Dee could still see denim material covering it. The creature turned and looked up at Dee.

It let out a high-pitched shriek and jumped up and down. The feeding frenzy below stopped. All the creatures glanced up and howled. Jeans dropped its meal and, with an astonishing leap, landed in the tree. Dee hacked at it with the machete, but it dodged the blows as it hissed at her.

"Go!" she yelled at the kids." Get in the river."

Crack! Crack!

Gunshots rang out, distracting Dee. Jeans struck out its claws at her, missing her by a whisker as she ducked just in time. More gunshots followed the first two in quick succession. The creatures below looked around in confusion as they began to drop like flies.

Jeans shrieked at Dee, baring its mouth. She gasped as she caught a glimpse of its tiny sharp teeth. Grunting, Dee swung the machete and connected with a blow to the side of the neck. The blade was sharp and dug in deep, finally silencing the creature.

Dee glanced up as two men, rifles nestled into their

shoulders, approached. From the way they walked and swept their rifles from side to side, she assumed they were military.

The two men killed the last of the feeding beasts and, while one took up a covering position, the other looked up at Dee.

"Evening, Mam."

"Hey."

"How many are with you?"

"Three," Dee said. "Children."

The army man nodded. "Sergeants Holt and Bawden." He clicked in a fresh magazine. "We should go before that pack gets wind of us."

"Go where?" Dee said, frowning.

"Claudelands. We're evacuating everyone out of the cities."

"Why there?"

"Less questions. More moving. Let's go."

Dee waved to the kids and helped them as they climbed down and into the arms of Sergeant Holt.

— 9 —

There was a strange smell of rotting fruit as Jack tiptoed over the wooden floorboards. He could never understand the appeal of that choice of flooring. Too noisy in his opinion. He made it to the kitchen without seeing anything suspicious. The house was clean and tidy, like whoever had lived here had never returned home when the news broke. Next to the internal door that led to the garage, the owners had kindly mounted a keypad.

Jack smiled. That saved him a lot of time hunting. He snatched up the keys for the Toyota Hilux and pocketed them.

"You hungry, grumpy boy?" Emma said, opening kitchen cupboards. She pulled several boxes of muesli bars and crackers from the shelves and placed them on the counter.

"Grab it and let's go," Jack said. "I want to be on the water asap."

"Here." Emma threw Jack a box of protein bars. He caught them and shoved them into his backpack.

Jack pressed the door release again and frowned. He tried the light switch, checking to see if there was electricity. It blinked on and bathed the garage in a soft glow.

He tried the release button again with no luck. Giving up, Jack pulled the manual override cord and strained as he lifted the large garage door. Besides the new Toyota, the owner had a couple of 1970s muscle cars. Jack let out a whistle. Even though he wasn't a car person, he knew the value of the machines. He chuckled wryly to himself.

Not anymore.

Jack busied himself. First, he manoeuvreed the Toyota to the boat trailer. Next, he wound down the trailer and mounted it to the tow bar. He didn't bother attaching the electrics.

"Why don't we just take the 4x4?" Emma said, munching on a muesli bar.

"Because those things hate the water," Jack mumbled. "I tried driving; the roads were crazy yesterday. I'd hate to get stuck in some gridlock. We wouldn't stand a chance."

"Okay. How are we getting around Karapiro?"

"Driving," Jack said, grunting as he clicked the shackle closed. "Ready? Let's go."

Jack had opened the door to the Toyota when he heard the noise. He paused and reached for his bachi hoe. He strained his ears. It wasn't a howl or a shriek. As it drew closer, he could make out the distinctive sound of V8 engines tearing down the road. He glanced at Emma and flicked his head at the house. She nodded, understanding.

Until they knew who these people were, they weren't going anywhere. Jack shut the front door as the noise of the V8 engines grew louder. A bright red Holden

Commodore screeched to a stop and skidded into the driveway.

Jack peeked through the curtains and watched as four men climbed out of the car. They were dressed in blue jeans, T-shirts and leather jackets. They were all armed with assault rifles. Jack had no idea what kind or what they were capable of. He had always thought those kinds of guns were unavailable in New Zealand.

The driver stretched his back and slung his rifle over his shoulder. He ambled up to the door, skipping a few steps along the way, and knocked once, twice, three times.

"Little pig. Little pig. Let me in."

Jack could feel his heart slamming in his chest. His tired mind swam with thoughts. But the one that shouted the loudest was *Why? Why were these men here?*

He glanced back at Emma and gestured towards the back of the house.

"Little pig? Are you there?" the driver shouted this time, anger lacing his tone. "Tell you what. We just want the girl. You can go free." The driver cackled. "Good luck out there."

Jack crouched down next to Emma and leaned in closer so that his mouth was next to her ear. "On the count of three, we're going to run out that ranch slider and into the trees. Keep running. Don't look back, all right? Head for the river."

Emma nodded and glanced at the front door.

"Last chance, Chief," the driver said. "I'll give you to the count of three."

Jack tightened his grip on his bachi hoe.

"One!" The front door smashed open, slamming into

67

the wall. Boots thumped on the floor as the driver and his three companions stormed into the room. Within seconds, Jack and Emma were surrounded.

Jack dropped his weapon and held his hands up. He and Emma were roughly hauled to their feet. Emma struggled and winced as her arm was twisted behind her back.

Jack turned and faced the driver. "What do you want?"

"I told you, Chief," the driver said. "Her."

He looked up at his men and smiled before looking back at Jack. "You. I don't need. Kill him."

"Wait!" Jack pleaded. "C'mon man. I'm just trying to get home to my wife. Please let me go."

Jack glanced at Emma, trying to convey that he wouldn't let them take her. That he would find her and help. She was struggling against the man who was holding her, but for once remained quiet.

"They call me Duke. Tell you what, Chief, I'll give you a one-minute head start. If you can evade my men, you'll be on your way and home to your wife."

Jack frowned and looked at the other three men. They were dressed for a chase. If he could make it to the river, he knew he stood a chance.

As he stood there facing Duke, Jack ran the plan through his head.

Evade these assholes.

Circle back.

Rescue Emma.

Go home.

Problem was, they had guns. Real guns. Not just some vermin pea shooters. Real military rifles. He hesitated and looked at Emma.

She smiled and nodded. "Go, Jack. I'll be okay."

He watched her for a few moments, trying to gauge the sincerity of her words. Finally he turned back to Duke. Duke was watching him, a big grin spread over his face.

"One minute?" Jack said.

Duke crossed his heart. "Promise. One whole minute."

"Okay."

"You better run, Chief," Duke laughed. "Clock is ticking."

Jack pushed past the men holding Emma. "Sorry," he whispered as he went past. Jack made for the back of the house before pivoting and sprinting out the front door.

The only plan he had come up with involved the speedboat. Laughter followed him as he jumped into the 4x4 and tore out of the driveway, pulling the boat. It had been a long time since he had driven down this road, but he was certain of a boat ramp at the beginning of Lake Karapiro.

Faster he urged the vehicle on, constantly glancing in his mirrors, checking for pursuit. By his reckoning he had perhaps thirty seconds left and still there was no sign of the lake or the boat ramp.

Something glinted in the side mirror a fraction before a bullet pinged off the 4x4. Jack ducked and frantically looked around for the shooter.

Another bullet pinged off the metal. Jack cursed himself. Why had he expected Duke to keep his word?

He caught a glimpse of the lake through the trees as he whizzed by. Slowing down, Jack took a deep breath and wrenched the wheel, aiming for a narrow one-lane road.

The Toyota bounced and fishtailed around as he struggled to regain control.

At least they've stopped shooting.

Lake Karapiro was spread out in front of him as he desperately searched for a way to get the boat into the water quickly. He glanced left and right. He soon realised there was no way he could launch the craft: the terrain was simply too steep. He needed to lose the boat, and fast.

Jack brought the 4x4 to a halt and leapt from the vehicle. V8 engines growled on the wind. Duke and his men were getting close. Jack wiped his sweaty hands on his hiking shorts and peered around the back of the Toyota. Duke's vehicle and three others were hurtling towards him. Men were leaning out of the windows, guns raised in the air.

Jack sighed and blinked away tears. He hated to leave Emma to whatever horrible fate these men had in mind for her, but he had to think of himself. Of Dee. She meant everything to him, and Jack wanted nothing more than to see her beautiful blue eyes again. To hold her. Feel the safety of her arms wrapped around him.

He glanced at the dark water of the lake and cast his eyes across to the other side. He could see houses. Perhaps he could shelter there.

With one last look back at Duke and his men, Jack grabbed his hiking pack and dived into the lake, gasping as the cold water embraced him.

Here we go again.

— 10 —

"Single file. Follow Bawden. Keep silent," Holt said. "Understood?" He stared at Dee, waiting.

"Understood. But I'm going home. I'm waiting for my husband."

"Negative. All civilians are to be evacuated." Holt grabbed her arm and pushed her in front of him.

She bit her lip and decided to play along for a while. They were heading in the direction of her house and, more importantly, away from the creatures.

Holt thumbed the radio he had strapped onto his tactical vest.

"Four civvies for extraction," Holt said.

There was a moment of static before a garbled voice rippled over the airwaves. "Negative. Holt...they're everywhere. Go!" The popping sounds of gunfire filtered through.

"Say again, Nikau?"

"Creatures..." *Crack! Crack!*

Holt tried to reach Nikau a couple more times, but to no avail. He turned back to Dee, his brow furrowed. "Looks like we're walking. What's the quickest route to Claudelands Arena?"

"Follow this river trail for about three kilometres until we reach the rail bridge. Cross that and we'll nearly be there," Dee said.

He nodded and tapped Bawden on the shoulder. The two soldiers had a brief, hushed conversation before taking up positions, Bawden in front of the children and Holt just behind Dee.

Bawden led them back onto the paved riverpath. He swivelled his rifle constantly from side to side, his eye glued to the scope on the back. Dee had only seen equipment like that in one of Jack's action movies.

After the golf course, the path ascended steeply, hugging the limestone cliffs that edged this stretch of the river. Expensive mansions perched precariously atop the cliffs, overlooking the water. Dee could hear the occasional scream, shout and the odd crying out. But, other than that, there were no other human sounds. No cars. No music. Not even the usual night-time squawk of birds or hoot of the morepork. The howls and shrieks of the creatures had taken over, every screech reminding her of the nightmare.

Bawden came to a sudden stop and held up his fist. He stopped so quickly, the children banged into his stumpy frame. He crouched down on one knee and signalled Holt, waving his finger and pointing ahead into the gloom.

Dee looked to where he was gesturing and cringed at the sight of a dozen pairs of yellow glowing eyes. The eyes blinked as one, and a hideous shriek rattled Dee's brain. Chaos broke out as everything happened at once.

Holt and Bawden aimed their carbines into the mass of yellow eyes and began firing. Over the din of the gunfire, Holt screamed at her, "Get the kids out of here!"

The eyes morphed into creatures as they flitted out of the dark and bounded towards the humans. Bawden and Holt were dropping them as fast as they could, but every time they killed one, another took its place.

Dee was rooted to the spot, paralysed by indecision. The only way out was up. Up through the scrub and through the grounds of the mansions. The children began screaming as they spotted the beasts. Dee snapped out of her immobility and picked up the nearest kid. She struggled over the flimsy wire fence, turned, and helped the other two children over. Holt glanced back and shouted something, his words lost in the commotion. Dee pushed the children in front of her, urging them on through the scrub. Behind her, the gunfire became sporadic before falling silent as she made it into the back yard of a house. It gleamed in the moonlight, its bright white paint shining like a beacon. They made it up onto the deck and huddled against the house, gasping for breath. Dee hugged the children close. She still had the machete and turned it over in her hands. Its blade and handle were pitted and chipped. She listened to the sounds of the beasts and twisted the weapon in her hands. She looked down at the children as they hugged her tight, frightened. Dee sighed. What use was this machete if two highly trained soldiers with assault rifles couldn't make it.

She knelt down next to the kids. "I don't live too far away. We're going to find a car and go there, okay?"

The children whimpered but didn't speak. Dee didn't blame them. If she paused to admit it, she was terror-stricken to the point of giving up. The sights and sounds of Rachel, Machete and Broomstick being eaten would haunt her for the rest of her life.

Dee had a sudden image of Jack flit through her mind. He was wearing his hiking pack and he was smiling. Those blue eyes that seemed to smile at her, no matter his mood. One of his favourite sayings, something he'd tried to instil in her, flashed through her mind.

There is always a way out.

Dee stood and gazed down at the river. She could see the glow of fires on the other side as she tried to get her exact bearings. By the way the crow flies, she was still two kilometres from home. Three by the streets.

She gritted her teeth and took the smallest child's hand. "No noise, okay?"

For the second time that night, Dee crept around the side of a house, heart pounding, fingers tingling with fear. Gripping the machete tight, whitening her knuckles, she led the kids away from the mansion, keeping to the shadows. She marvelled at how the children didn't make a sound, at how they were allowing her, a complete stranger, to guide them. Trusting her. Dee just hoped she had made the right decision. Common sense told her to get inside one of these houses and wait until daylight, but Dee wanted the familiarity of her own house.

Once there, she had access to a month's-worth of food and water. She had a katana and the basement could be easily secured. Better that than going into the unknown.

Dee and the kids ducked behind a car that had slammed into a power pole. Glass and oil covered the ground. Tentatively, Dee looked inside and smiled at the sight of the keys hanging from the ignition.

"Lady?" A kid tugged on her arm and pointed across the road. Dee froze when she spotted the creature. All the hair on its head had fallen out except for a wispy clump near its forehead. It reminded her of some of those bad haircuts back in the 90s. She reached behind and nudged at the children, gesturing at them to get into the car. Dee cracked the door open, all the while keeping an eye on the beast. For now, it seemed intent on sniffing the driveway opposite. Once the kids were in the car, she edged around the front of the vehicle.

Unfortunately Dee was too busy watching the creature and not keeping an eye on where she was placing her feet. Glass crunched under her feet, cracking like she was walking on eggshells.

The beast's head snapped up and swivelled around. It locked onto Dee in a split second and let out a bloodcurdling shriek. Dee cursed and sprinted to the driver's door. Within seconds the creature barrelled into her, knocking her into a garden. She braced herself for the beast to start tearing her flesh, but no pain came. No snarls. No shrieks. No agony.

Dee shook her head and brought the machete up, looking for the beast. It lay slumped on the grass verge with what looked like an arrow sticking out of its head.

Dee took a step back when she saw a man dressed in black army fatigues and holding a bow walking towards her. He gestured with his head to get into the vehicle, and held the door open for her. Without a word, Dee slid into the passenger seat. The mystery man started up the car and pulled away.

Only once they were several blocks away did he speak. "Where to?"

"Sorry?"

"Where do you want me to drop you and the kids off?"

Dee glanced back at the kids huddled in the back seat. "Can you take these kids to Claudelands?"

"To the evac site?"

"Yes," Dee said. "They're not mine. Please make sure they are safe."

"What about you?"

"Turn right here. My house is not far."

"You should evacuate too. It's only going to get worse."

"Thank you. But I'm not going anywhere without Jack."

"Fair enough," Mystery-man said. "Crazy, but your funeral."

"What about you?" Dee said, raising her eyebrow.

The man glanced out the window, at the houses lying dark and silent. Cars abandoned.

"I don't play well with others. Best if I'm on my own."

Dee held out her hand. "Dee."

The man shook it. "Jimmy."

"Thank you for saving us back there, Jimmy," Dee said. "Can I trust these kids into your care."

Jimmy turned and looked Dee in the eye. Dee saw a jagged scar on his cheek, running from his eye to his jawline. He reached into his shirt pocket, pulled out a leather wallet and handed it to Dee.

She flipped it open and smiled. Jimmy was a police detective. Homicide division.

"Don't worry, Dee. I'll get the kids to the evac site."

"Okay. Thanks."

Dee let her misgivings go. After that incident back when she'd been a teenager, she'd been wary of people, finding it difficult to trust anyone.

For the first time since she had left Rachel, Dee had hope as she directed Jimmy to her house. After waving the kids off, she bolted the door behind her and ran through the house checking all the windows were latched, though she doubted even those would hold the creatures out if they came. If the virus turned every infected person into one of those beasts, then everyone was doomed.

Dee glanced at the internal door that led down into the basement and garage. She would move down there tomorrow, but not before using the last of the hot water on a shower.

Grabbing her katana from above the fireplace, she headed to the bathroom. Tears flowed and quickly became sobs as memories of Rachel dying flicked through her mind.

— 11 —

Bullets zipped past and over him, landing harmlessly in the lake. Jack crouched lower and waded through the reeds that choked the shoreline, doing his best to keep out of sight. Duke and his men may have had fancy assault rifles, but they couldn't aim to save themselves.

After another ten minutes, they gave up and drove off. Jack glanced around at the nearest house but decided it was too obvious; they were probably heading there now to set up and wait to pick him off as he left the safety of the bushes.

Instead, Jack headed for the narrowest point of the lake and, using a side-stroke motion so he could hold his pack above his head, swam across. He half-expected Duke and his men to take pot shots but thankfully it seemed like they had lost interest and decided to leave him to the creatures that prowled the countryside.

Ten minutes later, Jack crawled out of the lake and sank gasping onto the muddy bank. He spent a few minutes getting his breath back and rehydrating. As he scoffed a protein bar, he spied a mountain bike leaning against a woodpile a few metres away.

His brilliant plan of escaping by boat and rescuing

Emma had come to nothing. His stomach tied itself in knots as he imagined what Duke and his men were going to do to her. It pained him that he was helpless, just one man against several heavily armed lunatics.

I'm sorry, Emma.

Jack slipped on his pack and jumped on the bike. In seconds he was pedalling down the road, his ears straining for any sounds of V8 engines. There were plenty of trees and bushes to hide in if Duke and his men came looking. He glanced up at the sun as it lowered in the sky and figured he needed shelter, fast. He couldn't risk being out in the open for much longer. It was nearly twenty-four hours since he'd called Dee and been told of the virus. Twenty-four hours of chaos. He shook his head. A trip that normally would have only taken him fifty minutes had turned into a crazy nightmare.

Jack cast his mind back to the hut, to the message. To Flatcap and his family. His first sighting of the creatures. His escape down the river and finding Emma. He had survived when others hadn't. And his aim of getting home to Dee was all that was keeping him going.

Jack sighed and began searching for somewhere to shelter. Distant howls reminded him of the creatures that now plagued the land. He had hoped to at least reach Cambridge and the evacuation centre today. Maybe they had records on who had made it out of Hamilton.

He pedalled on, scanning the countryside and buildings as he went. He saw plenty of houses but wanted to avoid them if he could. He needed somewhere with thick concrete walls, something he could barricade.

After twenty minutes, Jack spotted the green weatherboard buildings of a small country school. He slowed down and brought the bike to a halt.

He mulled over his options. Most of these older schools had boiler rooms and hidden passages. Perhaps he could lock himself in one of the rooms.

He glanced around the car park and noticed a white minivan but no other vehicles. Out of habit, a recently evolved one, he checked the ignition for keys but came up short.

Jack wheeled his bike out of sight and headed for the administration block. Peering in the window, he gasped at the sight of a blonde-haired woman reading a book to a young boy with bright red hair. She glanced up, noticed Jack and protectively moved the boy behind her. Her eyes flicked to the door a few metres to Jack's right. He held up his hands to show her that he was unarmed and kept eye contact with her as he approached the door.

"Hi," Jack said as he entered, keeping his tone non-threatening. "I'm Jack."

The woman watched him as he closed the door behind him. She looked him up and down, her eyes settling on the bachi hoe. "Sarah and George."

Jack stayed by the door with his hands up. "I'm just looking for somewhere to shelter for the night, then I'll be off at midday."

"Why midday?" Sarah frowned.

"Those creatures seem to disappear for a few hours around then."

Sarah relaxed a little at his explanation. Jack could see George peeking out from behind her legs, smiling widely at him.

"I thought everyone must have headed off to the evacuation centre," Jack said. "I've hardly seen anyone."

Jack wanted to warn them about Duke and his men but decided to wait for the right moment rather than frighten them now.

"Evacuation centre?" Sarah said.

"It's in Cambridge, at the race course. You didn't know?"

"No." Sarah shook her head. "I can't get anything else on my radio. Just the same message; to go to your nearest CD safe zone." Sarah gestured around the room.

Jack realised he had been focused on Sarah and George. It was only now that he noted the contents of the room. From the look of the couches and chairs, the small kitchenette with a coffee machine, bookshelves full of books, it had to be the staff room. Sarah and George had made a little nest of blankets and pillows on one of the bigger couches.

"I'm one of the teachers here, so when I heard the broadcast, I grabbed as much food as I could and headed down here. We keep plenty of supplies at the school in case of a natural disaster. I thought it would be the best place to wait it out."

"Good idea," Jack said, nodding.

"Where are you heading, Jack?"

"Hamilton," Jack said. "I've been trying to get home for the last twenty-something hours but it's…" Jack glanced down at George and back to Sarah. He gave her a slight shake of his head.

"Bad out there, is it?"

"It's been quite the journey so far, yeah."

A howl echoed through the school, interrupting their conversation.

Sarah looked at her watch and back to Jack. "Lock that

door and follow me," she said.

She took George by the hand and led Jack to the back of the staff room, through a sliding door and into a small supply room beyond. Once they were in, she slid the door across and snapped shut a bolt that had been hastily installed. Jack helped her shift a couple of chairs and wedged them tight against the door.

Finally, Sarah lifted a trapdoor open and pointed. "It will be a tight squeeze but it's all we have."

"Anything is better than being out there with them."

Sarah settled George onto a single mattress as Jack looked around. His theory about the school having maintenance tunnels for the old boiler system was correct. The concrete was aged and covered in stains, the air thick with the stench of diesel and oil, long since gone. Sarah had done her best to make the space more liveable with an air freshener, blankets and pillows. There was a gas-powered camping lantern and George had colouring books and crayons. Some of the pictures he had drawn were hung on the wall.

"How long have you been hiding here?"

"This will be night three," Sarah said. She reached past him and secured another bolt across the trapdoor.

Jack laid his pack down next to him and stretched out his legs as best he could. Sarah was right, it was a tight squeeze. Especially for his 6ft 2-inch frame. He could hear the muffled howls of the creatures and rubbed his hand over the handle of his bachi hoe, waiting for the beasts to break in and attack. But it remained silent above him.

Sarah offered him water and took a sip out of her own bottle. "What's in Hamilton that you are so eager to get back too?"

"Dee." Jack smiled, sipping his water. "My wife." He turned, blinking away tears. The thought of her worrying about his well-being and him not being able to contact her was driving him nuts.

Jack took another mouthful of water. "I was hiking up in the Kaimais. I've been trying to get home since yesterday. But the roads are all blocked. I got this far mainly by river. That's how I discovered that the creatures disappear around midday."

"I'm thinking of heading to this evac centre in Cambridge tomorrow with George. I can give you a lift if you want?" Sarah said.

"It's worth a look. We'll have to be careful, though."

"I thought you said the creatures disappeared?"

"It's not them I'm worried about."

Sarah eyes widened. "What is it?"

"I won't give you the details. Let's just say, men with guns."

Sarah glanced down at George, who was drawing something on a piece of paper, and ran a hand through her hair, twisting it in her fingers as she glanced back at him.

Jack didn't blame her. Most people would be worried about just surviving. Surviving the creatures. Staying alive. Having enough food and water and keeping your loved ones safe.

But Jack had seen countless movies and read hundreds of post-apocalyptic novels. After the initial shock of the event, once the survivors had learned to deal with the monsters, it always came down to the human factor. Humanity was a strange beast. Capable of great kindness, great industry and great determination. But, at the same time, capable of great evil.

A quote he often thought of came to mind. *To have one, you must have the other.*

To his movie-geek mind that meant a balance in the force. Yin and yang. But, more often than not, evil and the machinations of men resulted in situations like this.

"What do you think happened out there?" Jack said.

"With the virus?" Sarah asked as she wriggled her legs and pulled a woollen blanket over them, trying to make herself comfortable. She shrugged.

"Dee, my wife, said it started in America and spread out within a few days?"

"Something like that," Sarah said. "The first I heard of it was on the morning news. It showed some crazy scenes of people running in Chicago, I think. We discussed it here in the staff room that day but no one thought it was anything bad. I just thought it was crazy America again."

"Crazy America?"

"Well, I mean, in the way their news is. Not the country itself," Sarah said. She looked down at George, who was happily colouring his picture. "I'm glad I don't teach over there though. All those shootings."

Jack nodded. "I could use some of their assault rifles about now though." Jack looked at her. "What made you come here?"

"It was a couple of days later, on Friday I think. News alerts started with reports of the virus in Auckland, and then it spread to Wellington, Christchurch, Dunedin. Schools were closed, and by the evening the Civil Defence started telling everyone to stay inside and lock their doors. Or get to their nearest safe zone."

Jack raised his eyes and rubbed his thumb and forefinger over his chin. His mind was racing as he tried to figure out the timeline of events. A virus that spread that fast and caused that much disruption was insane. He looked over at George and Sarah. They were lucky, extremely lucky to have made it so far.

The sound of glass breaking clattered above him. He snapped his mouth shut, stopping the question he had for Sarah from leaving his lips. Her eyes found his and she raised a finger to her mouth. George had gone rigid, his eyes flickering around the small space.

Sarah placed a pair of earmuffs over his head and hugged him tight, covering him in her blanket.

They were dead-quiet. All Jack could hear was the sound of their breathing. He gritted his teeth and glanced at the bolt, hoping it would hold.

He listened for a few more minutes, but apart from the shattering of glass, no other sounds came. Sarah shut off the lantern, plunging the tiny space into darkness.

Jack shifted off his injured leg and shut his eyes. There was nothing to do now but wait. Wait, and hope that tomorrow he could finally find his way home to Dee.

— 12 —

Jack rolled his shoulders, trying to warm up his aching muscles. It had been a long, sleepless night in the maintenance tunnels with Sarah and George. Every creak, every tap, had woken him. The fear of the creatures discovering their hideout had kept him from getting any more than a few minutes of sleep.

Jack checked his watch. It was finally nearing midday.

"Ready?" Jack said.

"Okay," Sarah said, and helped George into a jacket. "Straight to my minivan?"

"Yes."

When they hadn't been able to sleep, Jack had borrowed some of George's paper and written down what he thought they should do. Sarah had agreed about going to the evac centre, but her next question had been "What if?"

Jack had to admit that he thought there would be soldiers and officials there waiting for any stragglers. But what if no one was there? He had explained to Sarah about his cabin filled with supplies, tucked away from civilisation. The conversation went back and forth as Sarah tried to decide whether to go with Jack or try to reach family in the Bay of Plenty. After Jack had told her about the state of the main roads, she'd agreed to come with him and Dee.

Sarah nodded to him, indicating she was ready, and Jack carefully slid the bolt back, cringing with every squeak it made. As he lifted the trapdoor, he half expected one of the creatures to howl and sink its teeth into the top of his head. He still had the bachi hoe, but in the cramped space it would have been almost useless. Slowly he lifted the door higher, blinking in the bright sunlight that bathed the room above. He could see the broken glass from several windows and muddy scuff marks, but there was no sign of the creatures.

Jack hesitated halfway out, his mind casting back to the day before, to Duke and his men. He glanced down at Sarah and, taking a calming breath, lifted himself clear. After checking his surroundings, Jack was satisfied they had gone undiscovered. Sarah had chosen her foxhole well. The creatures had been here during the night, but thankfully, for whatever reason, they had moved on, searching for easier prey.

It was warm and sunny as Sarah drove them towards Cambridge. Jack swivelled his head from side to side as they whizzed past dairy farms and horse studs. He smiled to himself at the dozens of studs. If there was one thing Cambridge was well-known for, it was breeding thoroughbred horses. Jack thought about getting Sarah to stop so he could check to see if he could find a shotgun or two, but now that he was within twenty kilometres of Dee, he wanted to get there as soon as possible.

Ten minutes later, they entered the outskirts of the

town and Sarah slowed the minivan to a crawl. Ahead of them, the street was littered with debris. Cars were parked haphazardly, some with doors open and engines running. One or two had stereos on, playing garbled music. Next to the cars were pools of blood, some fresh and red, others older and dark.

George gasped behind them. "Mummy!" he cried.

"Don't look, George. Close your eyes. Okay, hun?"

Jack looked over his shoulder at the red-haired boy. He was still staring out the window, eyes wide. Taking it in.

Sarah had to weave the car around a few vehicles that had collided, scattering shattered glass across the road. Doors to several houses were open, their contents dispersed into gardens. Jack blew out a whistle at all he was seeing. It was panic. Chaos and panic. Those not infected by the virus had tried to flee, only to be caught by the creatures.

Sarah brought the minivan to stop and groaned. The narrow bridge ahead of them that spanned the Waikato River was jammed, making it impassable. This had been their last chance; they had tried the other two bridges already.

"That's the last bridge for miles," Sarah said. "Looks like we're walking."

"Let's make it quick. The race course is about a ten minute walk from here."

"I'll carry George if you take my bag," Sarah said.

Jack hefted his hiking pack over his shoulders and tightened the straps, making sure it was secured. Next, he hooked Sarah's pack over his left shoulder so that he still had movement on his right. Enough to swing the bachi hoe if needed. He glanced at the sun and figured that they still had an hour at least before the beasts emerged.

Sarah lifted George to her chest and hugged him tight so his face was against her chest. She nodded that she was ready and Jack moved out and across the bridge. All the vehicles were empty of people, though their belongings remained, some spilled out on the ground. Jack picked up a couple of water bottles and the odd chocolate bar. As silently as they could, they skirted the main shopping area, taking a smaller side street that went around behind the shops. His nerves felt like a thousand needles stabbing him as he scanned the vicinity for the monsters, and for people like Duke. Jack didn't ease the pace until they could see the evac centre up ahead.

As soon as he saw the race course, Jack knew something was wrong. It was the lack of movement. The lack of noise. Now that there was no one around, the ambient noise of human civilisation that always played in the background was absent. Surely they should've heard something, anything, as they approached?

He gently tugged at Sarah's arm and ducked behind a row of trees. "Stay here," he said." It's too quiet. I'll go on and check it out."

Moving as quietly as possible, Jack flitted through the woods from tree to tree, staying in the shadows and keeping the trunks between himself and the evac centre. Dark green army tents had been set out in rows. Interspersed between them were white medical tents with red crosses. Careful to not be seen, he crept up behind one of the tents and ducked in. Jack gasped at the sight that greeted him. Cots, blankets and clothing were jumbled about like a bull had gone crazy. Broken cups and glasses lay everywhere.

The same scene played over and over as Jack moved through the camp. Everything was chaos. Everyone had either run for their lives or been taken by the beasts. This wasn't an evacuation centre; it was an extinction centre. Jack spotted a rifle lying next to a medical tent and jogged over. The stench coming from inside nearly overpowered him. When he ducked his head in, he saw beds, some empty and some containing people. Jack clamped a hand over his mouth to prevent himself retching. One of the infected was thrashing about on its bed, its skin blackened, bleeding from its eyes and ears. Jack scooped up the rifle and started to jog back to Sarah. As he ran, he kept an eye out for a vehicle. Jack was tired of running. Tired of this endless quest to reach Hamilton and the safety of Dee. He knew that if he could just reach Dee, everything would be okay. Dee had that way about her. She made you feel safe, feel that anything was possible.

Jack heard the throaty V8s rumbling up the road before he saw them. Duke. He cursed to himself. Of course that asshole would come sniffing around here. Probably after more guns and whatever drugs he could find.

Jack crouched down behind a tent and looked over his pilfered rifle. He recognised it as something the NZ Army used, but beyond that, he had no clue. He had no idea how to use it. He tried to recall what Dee had shown him with her dad's guns. Surely they were similar? It didn't take him long to find the safety switch. It had three settings. Safety, semi, and full. He clicked it to semi and tested pushing it into his shoulder. Apart from a shotgun, he had never fired a weapon before.

You'd better learn fast.

Duke and his men tore into the evac centre, three cars skidding their tyres in the mud. They each drove around in a circle, revving their engines. Jack cringed, fearful of the noise they were making. Fearful of the creatures coming for them and fearful of being discovered. Duke had let him go last time only to hunt him. Jack knew that this time he would be executed on the spot.

He kept an eye on Duke from his hiding spot. The man raised a clenched fist from his car window, halting the maddening din. Even from this distance, Jack could hear his shouted orders.

"Todd. Take Pixie and Mac, gather up all the weapons the army has so kindly left us. Nancy-boy, you and Alan are on drug duty. And if I catch you taking any, I'll kill you myself. Jeff, we're on food."

The men exited their vehicles and walked away, leaving one person in Duke's car. Jack squinted trying to get a better look. Emma? What was she doing here?

Jack gritted his teeth. These men strutted about in such a carefree manner that Jack wondered if they knew about the creatures' habits at all. Not that he planned to educate them. He waited a few more minutes, listening to them as they plundered their way through the centre, crashing over unwanted supplies. The sounds reverberated around the race course, making him more nervous. Once they were far enough away, Jack rose and crab-walked to Duke's red Holden Commodore. Emma was looking away from him as he clicked open the door and held up his hand.

Emma snapped her head around, her eyes bulging in

surprise. She held up her hands, which had been cable-tied together and pointed to her feet.

Jack always carried a knife in his hiking pack. It was one of those objects that had so many uses, like duct tape. He made short work of the ties and tugged Emma through the car. They hugged briefly, Jack turned quickly, leading the way. It was easy to avoid Duke and his men. They made so much noise it was like a child care centre had been released in a toy shop.

Jack paused at the edge of the tents and glanced across the road. He could see Sarah's bright red jacket amongst the trees, could sense her watching. With one last glance behind him, he gestured to the trees, pushing Emma in front of him. Jack clutched the rifle and followed her.

— 13 —

Thump!

Dee shuddered and risked a peek out the window. She had boarded up the windows as best she could, using every available scrap of timber and furniture. Anything to barricade herself in and keep the creatures out. So she only had a slither of a gap available to watch for Jack. She reached out and gently pulled the curtain aside. Her view was limited, but she could see the driveway and gate. Both led to the street.

Thump!

There it was again. Dee clenched her teeth and scanned the property, still seeing nothing. It was a bright sunny day, hardly a cloud in the sky. Dee loved autumn days like this. The last remnants of summer hanging on before the dreary winter set in. Seeing nothing, Dee let the curtain fall and relaxed the grip she had on her katana.

Still reeling from losing Rachel, and barely making it home, she tried to make herself safe. She'd fortified her house and boxed up all her provisions. She and Jack had prepared bug-out bags months ago. As she waited, Dee busied herself checking and rechecking the bags. It was two days since she had spoken to Jack, and with each passing hour the fear that she might have lost him gnawed at her more and more. She'd been out in that bedlam twice now, taking the risk to bike back to Rachel's to retrieve her car. Having it home settled her, like she needed it. Knowing that she had an out mattered, a means of escape in case Jack didn't come home.

Dee checked the driveway and gate once again, glanced at the pile of supplies. She had noted the growing number of creatures. At first it had been just the odd one, still human-looking with tattered clothes hanging off them. As the hours passed and day turned to night, they had come out in ever-increasing numbers. Solitary creatures had begun to gather in packs, prowling down the street and sniffing the air. When they smelt something, they would emit a high-pitched shriek and bound across the property and into the house.

Dee cringed every time she heard glass breaking and the screams that followed. Once, in the early morning, she had heard the boom of shotguns. Even that hadn't lasted long. With nothing to do but wait, her mind wandered and she found herself imagining what had become of Jack. Two nights had passed since they'd last spoken, but still she found it difficult to accept that he wasn't coming back.

Dee sighed and checked her phone for the hundredth time. She had very little battery power remaining and only kept it on out of habit. She switched it off and slid it into her jeans pocket.

She decided to move down to the basement. It was more secure there, and easier to defend with only two entries: one leading from the kitchen and the other from the back yard. Dee strapped the katana over her back and lifted the first box. Better to do something than sit around waiting.

It took Dee half a dozen trips to move everything she needed down to the basement. Next, she emptied out the pantry of all the canned goods, the fruit she had preserved over the summer and all the dried foodstuffs. Once she had everything she thought she'd need, she decided to secure the access door from the kitchen. She found some of Jack's tools and put a dozen 80 mm screws through the door into the thick timber jambs. Thankfully the door was solid with no window.

She had just finished screwing the door shut when she heard the shriek. It was so loud it wailed around in her brain. Frantic, she scanned the kitchen, looking for somewhere to hide. She glanced at the back door, which was ajar. Could she make it to the basement?

There was another shriek. This time it was close, perhaps even down the side of the house. Gritting her teeth, she ducked into the only hiding spot available: the pantry. The handle of her katana knocked the spice rack over, spilling the contents all over the floor. She swore quietly and pulled the door closed behind her. The pungent aromas from the spices hung in the air around her, so Dee covered her mouth with her T-shirt and held her breath.

The clicking of a creature's claws across the kitchen tiles and the popping of its joints made her skin crawl. She gagged when the rotting fruit smell that seemed to hang around them reached her nostrils through the mix of spices. She squeezed her eyes shut and held the door closed with one hand. Sweat began to pool in the small of her back and behind her ears, saliva in her mouth.

All it would take for the creature to discover her was one peek in at where she was hiding, one whiff of her scent.

Crouched in the pantry, she listened to the beast. It scrambled around, knocking God-knew-what to the floor. It would stop in its destruction every few seconds to sniff at the air. Dee could hear each sniff, because it made the creature sound like an obese asthmatic trying to breathe. She gulped in her own breath, as quietly as she could, when the creature scratched at the door. She heard it sniff again, and it sneezed. Powerful sneezes, one after the other. It seemed to scramble away from the door, its clawed feet scraping on the smooth tiles. There was a shriek, and the creature crashed out of the kitchen.

Dee waited until she couldn't hear it anymore. She counted to ten, slowly. She peeked out of the pantry. Pots, pans, cups and plates lay smashed all over the floor. The spices she'd spilled had claw marks in them.

Something clicked. The creatures hunted mainly by scent. Twice now she had escaped their detection because of overpowering smells, once in the compost and now again with these spices. To have any chance of surviving in the basement, she would need to disguise her presence.

Dee dashed for the basement and bolted the door shut. Smiling, she took the seaweed plant-food off the shelf and poured its contents over the door and threshold.

That would have to do for now.

Hurry, Jack! Come home.

— 14 —

The liquidambar was one of the first deciduous trees to begin changing colour in autumn, and one of Jack's favourite trees. Its leaves would first turn a deep purple before turning red and falling to the ground. Jack jogged ahead through the leaf litter that covered the grass, releasing a peaty scent into the air. He held the gun in front of him, ready. He remembered reading about where to keep your finger so as not to accidentally fire the gun; on the trigger guard, not the trigger itself. He was tempted to flick the safety on, but with Duke and his goons in the vicinity and the fact that mid-afternoon was fast approaching, he was on edge.

"Where are we going, Jack?" Emma gasped beside him.

"We need a vehicle. Best place is a dealership," Jack said. He glanced behind to check on Sarah. She was lagging behind, carrying George. Emma followed his gaze and dropped back.

"Here, let me take him for a bit," Emma said, handing Sarah the bachi hoe and lifting the red-haired boy into her arms. She spent a few seconds adjusting his weight.

"Thanks," Sarah panted.

It was a long run back into the centre of Cambridge. Jack was aiming for a Toyota dealership he knew of next to a strip mall of fast food outlets. As they ran, Jack caught his reflection in the shop windows, hardly recognising himself, he was so dishevelled. He must've smelt just as bad. It was days since he'd showered, and the swims in the river wouldn't have helped matters. Jack blinked as he caught a movement in the glass. It flicked through his vision so fast he wasn't sure what he had seen.

Only instinct saved him. He was close enough to Emma and Sarah to pull them down behind a vehicle just as the creature bounded out of the house. It howled and pivoted, searching for the prey it had seen. Jack caressed the rifle and crawled in front of the two women and George. He could just see the top of its deformed head. The flesh on the skull had blackened and there was no hair at all. It leapt onto a brick fence and sniffed at the air. Its yellow eyes swivelled around and locked onto Jack. For a moment Jack thought the beast was going to bound off. Moving slowly, he brought the rifle up and squinted through the scope.

There was a blur of motion and the creature was sailing through the air. Jack sucked in a breath and pulled on the trigger. The rifle bucked into his shoulder as three shots ripped out, going wide. Jack pulled the trigger again as the creature landed on the concrete and swiped a claw at him, knocking the rifle from his grasp.

George cried out and Emma, gripping the bachi hoe in both hands, stepped in front of Sarah and George. The creature bowled into Jack, its mouth curled back to reveal rows of razor sharp teeth. Jack fell back with a thump and grabbed the creature's arms, desperate to keep it from tearing into his flesh. He kicked out at the beast but his efforts had no effect. He spotted the rifle only a couple of metres away.

"Emma! The gun."

The beast gnashed it sucker mouth together and globs of drool dripped onto Jack's face. He glanced at Sarah and George hiding under the car. He glanced at the trees lining the streets. Streets that would normally be filled with life, with people going about their daily lives. They all lay empty now. Anyone left alive was either hiding or had been evacuated. He grunted, trying to push the monster off him, and stared into its soulless eyes. The creature thrashed about with new fervour, dragging its clawed hands down Jack's arms. Jack was watching its mouth when it suddenly went rigid and blackish blood began to drip from its mouth.

Jack frowned, puzzled. He hadn't heard any gunshots or sensed any movement. Emma kicked the creature off him and held out a hand. He clasped it and she pulled him to his feet. He glanced down at the beast and saw the bachi hoe embedded in its back.

"Thanks." Jack scooped up the fallen rifle. This time he placed the strap over his shoulder.

Howls echoed around the houses.

"We need to move," he said. "To the river, and a boat."

"What about a car?" Emma said.

"Too late. We'll be safer out on the water."

He and Emma helped Sarah and George out from underneath the car. Sarah brushed dirt out of George's hair.

"There's a jet boat company down by the highway bridge."

Jack nodded and pivoted, trying to orientate himself.

They headed in the general direction of the river, jogging from car to car and ducking into gardens when they could. Anything to keep out of sight. The creatures' howls and shrieks filled the town like a hundred wolves had suddenly invaded and were hunting for food. Sarah led them on a zig-zag route through the town centre, ducking down alleys and behind buildings. Finally Jack glimpsed the river and spotted the bright red building Sarah had mentioned. Painted on the roof were the words "Cambridge Jet Adventures". Perfect if you were an adrenaline junkie and didn't mind nature whizzing by.

Jack gripped his rifle tighter and waited until the others had moved past him. The shrieks of the beasts were getting ever closer. During the course of their flight, Jack could have sworn he kept seeing them, but whenever he searched for them, they were absent. He had put it down to being exhausted and paranoid.

"Jack?" Emma broke into his thoughts.

"Sorry. Coming." He caught up to her.

"Daydreamer, huh?"

"Yeah. I just had this weird feeling that we are being herded."

"Herded?"

"I could see the creatures. They've been following us the whole time."

Emma paused and glanced around. "We'd better hurry then."

Jack peered through the scope on his rifle and scanned the yard of the boating company. Next to the shed were three large speed boats and a tractor. All painted bright red like the shed. Apart from the birds and the insects, nothing moved. He strained his ears, trying to judge where the howls were coming from, but the noise echoed around and bounced off the river, making it nearly impossible to discern a direction.

"What do you guys think?" Jack whispered. "We're going to make a bit of noise, so we need to do this fast."

"What's the plan?" Sarah said.

"I'll drive the tractor and back it up to the trailer. Get George inside. You and Emma hook it on and I'll drive it into the river. I'm not going to bother backing it. Just straight in. As soon as we are in, start the boat and unhook it from the trailer. If all goes well, we'll be motoring downriver to Hamilton in a few minutes."

"Keys?" Emma asked, raising an eyebrow. "They're not going to be just hanging in the ignition."

Jack grinned. "The tractor ones are there. As for the boat, there should be a switch and an ignition button."

"Shouldn't we check before charging in?" Sarah asked.

A high-pitched shriek rang out over the yard. Jack shuddered. He swung his carbine up and searched for its source. Perched on the roof of the engineering business next door were five creatures.

"Go! Now!"

Jack slung the rifle over his shoulder and sprinted for the tractor. He was halfway there when movement blurred in his peripheral vision. Creatures were pouring out from behind every building, howling and spitting, jumping up and down at the sight of their prey.

"Run for the river!" Jack screamed. He swung around and squeezed the trigger. The rifle bucked to life. Jack wedged it into his shoulder and sprayed bullets at the oncoming mass of creatures. He couldn't even begin to count them. There had to be one hundred or more. Emma ran to join him, swinging the bachi hoe. She was overrun in seconds, her screams piercing through his brain.

Jack risked a look over his shoulder. Sarah and George were still metres from the river with the beasts closing in fast. Jack spread his feet and held his finger down on the trigger, desperate to save them.

His weapon clicked empty as the first creature reached him. Jack swung the rifle at it like a baseball player and grinned as the stock smashed into his head. He dropped to one knee and swung again before the rifle was ripped out of his grasp.

Several beasts pinned him down but did not attack. Jack frowned. What were they doing?

He turned his head and bit his lip, watching as Sarah and George were similarly caught and held.

Then, through the forest of clawed limbs that had him pinned, Jack saw it. A creature like the others, but taller and broader. It had strange, bark-like skin, and bones protruded from its shoulders. It turned, as if sensing Jack's attention, and grinned.

The beast above Jack squirted a hot, stinging liquid into his face. Jack gasped and fought the waves of nausea that followed. It felt like an invisible hand was reaching inside his skull and squeezing his brain. Jack's last thought as he drifted into unconsciousness was:

Run, Dee! Run!

— 15 —

Dee peered out through the ventilation grating. The late afternoon sunlight shone through the beech trees bordering the back yard and dappled the lawn. She held her breath. Several of the creatures were moving around the yard, sniffing at the air. She stepped backwards a couple of feet, deeper into the shadows, fearful they would see her. The creatures took their time, sniffing, moving, pausing, sniffing. As they moved, popping sounds emanated from their bodies. She could see their veins through their translucent dark skin. Willing them to move on, she watched, terrified. Finally, they hopped on top of the fence and, shrieking, bounded off.

Letting out a breath, Dee nearly choked on the stench of sewage as she inhaled again. She had been down here in the basement for two days now and, after discovering the creatures had a heightened sense of smell, she had decided to really confuse them. The sewage took some getting used to, but anything was better than experiencing the same fate as Rachel, Machete, Broomstick and the two soldiers.

Dee took stock of her situation. She had about three

weeks' worth of food, maybe the same of water, and one weapon.

Thank God Jack bought me the katana in Japan that I'd been obsessing about. But will it be of any use against these nightmares?

She tried to remain calm, but her worry for her husband of three years was taking its toll. Not for the first time, she wondered whether to head on to the cabin without him or not. She remembered their first year together.

Nights spent in, cuddling on the couch, sharing their favourite movies and TV shows.

Talking late into the night about anything and everything.

Weekends spent in the wilderness exploring, sharing a love of nature. Learning, teaching each other.

Teaching what it meant to care for someone deeply. Learning tolerance of others and their situations.

Dee had thought it too late, too much of a princess fantasy to find that "one", but she had.

She had fought her demons, her insecurities, every day with Jack. Her anxiety got the better of her some days, causing her to stay inside, hiding from the world. Cocooning herself away.

One night, after a few drinks, Dee had opened up to Jack, poured her heart out. She had told him about all her demons. Jack had cried, pouring out his own heart and releasing his own.

That had been that golden moment, that moment told in all the fairy tales.

She knew that was it. Jack was "The One."

A popping sound caused Dee to look back out into the yard. One of the creatures was back. A straggler, maybe? It was staring straight into her neighbour's house, sniffing the air. The sound of its sucker mouth smacked, making her shiver.

She prayed that her elderly neighbour, Faye, was hidden. In her nineties, the woman never ceased to amaze Dee with her virility by still playing tennis and tending her garden.

The virus had taken over so fast, and with so much fury, that no one had had a chance. Before the phones had died, Dee had called Faye, telling her to hide with her, to wait for Jack. Faye had refused, saying that her family were on their way. They were going together to the evac centre at Claudelands. But after five days, nothing. No sign of anyone. Dee now wished she had insisted having seen what was going on out there for herself and barely escaping with her life.

The creature was still there, sniffing. It suddenly burst over the fence with incredible speed, shrieking. Dee heard the crash of glass breaking. Her heart sank.

Against her better judgement, she grabbed the only weapon she had — the katana — and dashed outside. She leapt over the short boundary fence.

Dee could see the smashed window. A horrifying noise came from inside the house. Peering in, she saw the creature standing over Faye's torn body, one of her arms clamped in its claws. Blood and gore dripping from its strange sucker mouth, it let out another shriek. More shrieks answered from close by, maybe a few houses down.

With blinding speed, the creature leapt at Dee.

Stumbling backwards, she brought the katana up as she fell. The speed of the creature went against it as the tip of the sword slid in underneath its chin and up into its brain, killing it instantly. Black, foul-smelling sludge poured down the blade to coat Dee's arm and neck.

Gasping, her heart trying to beat its way out of her chest, she gagged and pushed the living nightmare off her. Hearing the shrieks again, but much closer, she listened intently. Screams, human screams, were intermingled with them.

Time to leave.

As she cleared the fence, she saw a group of people running up the street.

Dee gasped. *People? I haven't seen anyone for a couple of days!*

"In here!" she waved.

The group turned towards the sound of her voice as one, their eyes wide in terror. They changed course and dashed towards her.

Dee ran to her basement door and swung it open. Getting a better look at the group, Dee made out four men and a couple of women.

"Hurry! C'mon!" Dee called, gesturing urgently for them to get inside.

The shrieking sounded really close as she slammed the door behind them, bolting it.

"Quickly, in the back," Dee instructed. She reached into a plastic container and splashed some of the foul-smelling liquid over the door and floor.

Satisfied that she had disguised their presence, she joined the frightened group in the shadows. Dee could hear the creatures scratching around outside, and one of the creatures banged into the door, its joints popping as it moved around. It scratched at the door again, sniffing. Dee hoped that her seaweed garden solution would do the trick again, that its pungent stench would confuse the creatures, tricking them into thinking there was nothing to devour here. For the second time that day, the creatures moved on, and she breathed a sigh of relief.

"What's the awful smell?" asked one of the men, whispering. Dee looked at him. Shaved head, slightly overweight, funny, beady eyes.

"That awful smell just saved your life," Dee said. Annoyed, she met his eyes and glared at him.

"Matt, manners. She just saved our ass," said one of the women.

"Sheesh, all right."

Dee looked over at the woman who had chastised Matt and smiled. She had blonde hair, nice figure, a real beauty.

"Sorry about that. I'm Alice. You know Matt." She nodded in his direction. Pointing at the others, she listed their names in turn. "Mike, Aston, Vicki and Boss."

"Boss?" exclaimed Dee, looking closer at the teenage boy Alice had pointed at. "What, like Bruce Springsteen?"

Boss looked at Dee, a grin on his face. "Who?"

I like this kid already.

Boss started to laugh. "Nah, it's a gaming thing. I used to boss everyone around in my WOW guild, drove everyone nuts."

Oh, a gamer?

Dee grinned. "All right, Boss." Dee looked over the group and lowered her voice. "That foul smell is raw sewage. It hides our scent from those creatures out there. That stench I put on the door is seaweed, and it does the same thing. You are welcome to stay here, but I have rules. I've managed to hide away from the creatures for three days. You get used to it, trust me."

Dee glanced at each of them. So far they were paying attention.

"Rule one. Stay out of sight. Two. Minimal noise, no raised voices." Dee grimaced. "We can share what little food I have. Hopefully my husband Jack will arrive before we have to scavenge more."

"Variants. They're called Variants," murmured Boss.

Dee turned and looked at Boss. "What?"

"That's what the American on the radio was calling them. Variants."

"You've got a radio?"

"Well, had, until they found me and Mum."

Dee could see Boss didn't want to discuss the events of the last few days, so she made a mental note to ask him about it later.

Variants? Variants of what?

Dee's group settled into an uneasy routine. For ten days they tried their best to be silent at all times, especially during the night. The darkness brought nightmares of hellish proportions. The Variants outside scurried, popped and shrieked continuously.

The ever-present fear of being discovered frayed everyone's nerves. They took turns watching out of the ventilation grates in two-hour shifts, being careful to stay in the shadows.

Boss came up with the idea of dousing themselves in the seaweed solution, and Dee insisted that the human waste be buried and covered in garden lime. Minutes ticking by dragged into hours, and hours dragged into days.

And still no Jack.

With little else to do when not on watch, they played cards, read books from Jack and Dee's stored collection or tried to sleep. But, knowing what awaited them outside, real sleep was a forgotten luxury.

Boss and Dee became fast friends, finding a common ground in all things Monty Python. They would try to lighten their mood by writing quotes, each testing the other person's knowledge.

Matt, Alice and Aston all sat staring morosely, sometimes whispering to each other.

Vicki and Mike spent long hours just cuddling, only rising to do their shifts, eat and use the primitive bathroom. They had barely said two words to anyone, the shock of the past few days showing.

We all deal with things in a different way, some better than others.

Dee knew they probably had only one more days' worth of food left, at best. They had exhausted the supplies they'd managed to scrounge from the immediate neighbourhood. No one was willing to venture out any farther than they had already. A few close calls with the Variants had scared everyone. Now they had no choice. If they were going to eat, they would have to go out into the mess the virus had caused.

Looking up from the book she was reading, *The Chrysalids*, she nudged Boss with her foot. "Hey."

Boss was surrounded by electronic bits and pieces, remnants of an old ham radio her dad had given her. Without looking up, he replied, "Yeah?"

"Any luck?" Dee whispered.

"Nope, it's dead. An ex radio. Expired. No longer with

us." Boss was now grinning.

Playing along, Dee said, "It was all right when it left the shop." She sighed. "But seriously, could you fix it?"

"Not without the right parts. Then, yeah, maybe."

Dee leant forwards in her chair, shuffling closer to Boss. The smell of the dusty radio parts evoked fond memories of her childhood, of watching her father patiently assemble the old ham radio, trying to get it to work. He had explained what he was doing to Dee, but it had all sounded the same to her. She'd just loved hearing his voice.

Blinking away the memory, she furrowed her eyebrows at Boss. "So, did your father teach you how to do that?"

Boss paused. Putting down the small screwdriver, he shifted his weight, stretching out a leg. "Yeah, well, sort of. He taught me how to use the radio. He loved to chat to people all around the country, and the world too, I suppose. I don't know, really. He wasn't around much."

Dee watched as Boss shuffled around, turning away from her. He leant back down and picked up some pieces of the radio. He glanced around the room, his blue eyes flickering to her.

Dee placed a hand on his shoulder. "Boss, what happened? To him, to your mum?"

Wetting his lips, Boss said, "They happened, Dee. They!" He gestured wildly towards outside.

Dee patted his shoulder. "I'm sorry. I shouldn't have pried."

Boss sighed, rubbing his hands through his hair. He stared at Dee. "Dad worked as an IT consultant, hardware stuff. He mainly worked for that big animal breeding place. It wasn't long after the news broke, a couple of days maybe, that Dad came home sick. We thought he had a fever. He still insisted on going to work the next day, and then he never came back. As it got worse out there, Mum and I hid in the attic storage area. That's where Dad's radio was. So, when it was quiet, I warmed her up and reached out."

Dee rubbed the nape of her neck. "Is that when you talked to the American?"

"Yeah. It was difficult to hear him. He said something about Variants attacking them, and to hunker down."

Tilting her head in the direction of the others, Dee asked, "What about them? How'd you end up together?"

Boss picked up a piece of the radio. It was shaped like a small light bulb. Dee watched as he peered through it. He put it down next to the others and turned around to face her. His eyes glistened, and he blinked rapidly. "He came back, Dee. He came back."

Her heart thumped against her chest and nerves tingled down her arms, her blood ran cold. She shivered. She hoped that what he was going to say next wasn't what she was expecting. *Why did I press him?*

"After a few days, he came back. But he wasn't Dad any more. He was one of them, Dee!" His voice caught on the last words and tears welled up in his eyes.

"I ran, Dee. I ran, and left Mum to him." Boss sniffed and wiped his eyes. Gesturing towards Matt and Alice, he added, "They helped me. We hid in their shed. The other two were already there. But they found us. Then we met you." Boss sniffed again, and a smile escaped his lips.

Dee moved forwards off her chair. She swept a few of the scattered parts away with her foot and crouched down, joining Boss on the floor. She drew him into a tight embrace. "I'm really glad you did, Boss. We're going to survive this, okay?"

Boss tightened his arms around her, returning the hug. "Yeah. We better."

She held on to him for a while longer, savouring the comfort.

Dee thought about how to approach the next subject, that of the drastically dwindling food supply. She knew the average male needed three thousand calories a day to survive, and they were all on a thousand at best. The time had come. Judgement day.

She broke the embrace with Boss and sat back up on her chair. Not for the first time, she wished her dad was still alive. He'd always treated her with a love and affection that had sometimes bewildered her. She'd always known he'd really wanted a son. He'd taken her on several hunting trips and shown her how to live off the land. Firing hunting rifles and shotguns, fishing and camping had all been a big part of her life growing up. Dee cursed her luck at the Hemorrhage Virus arriving when the guns he'd left her were being serviced. His death had hit her hard, and she'd foolishly let the guns sit in the basement gathering dust. After Jack had shown some interest in learning how to use them, she had taken them in for servicing. Now they were lost to her too.

What should they do? Move on and maybe get torn apart and eaten, or stay put and starve to death, and maybe get discovered and eaten?

Where are you, Jack? I need you now, more than ever.

Shifting her weight, Dee nudged Boss again. "Boss."

"Yeah, what?"

"We need to talk to the others."

Slightly perplexed, Boss looked up from his task. "Why?"

"We need to figure out what we're going to do, that's why."

"Food?"

"Yes, food, and we need to move on. There are more and more Variants every day."

Getting up off the floor so he could sit next to her, Boss gave Dee a quizzical look. "Have you noticed how you don't see them in the middle of the day?"

Nodding, Dee murmured, "Yeah. I think that's our best chance to go. We need to find water, food and weapons. Real weapons, like guns. Jack and I have this cabin up in the valley, isolated. I think we should head there."

"What about a truck? Like a concrete truck?"

Smiling, Dee said, "We need to be practical, Boss. It's not Mad Max."

Stifling a laugh, Boss nodded. "All right. I'll gather the troops."

— 16 —

Dee smiled at Alice as she walked over. "We need to have a meeting, guys."

"Okay," Alice said, smiling back. "Over by the books?"

Dee nodded and listened as Boss talked to Mike.

"Hey, we're having a pow wow."

Mike turned his head away from the ventilation grate. "Why?"

"Same old, same old. Food, guns. Lack thereof," Boss whispered, tension creeping into his tone.

"Fine," Mike said, sighing. "What about the watch?"

"I'm just doing as Dee asked," Boss said, turning his back and shrugging his shoulders.

Grumbling and muttering, Mike went over to Vicki, and together they joined the others.

At a small table, Dee had spread out an old map of the city, and next to it, one of the surrounding countryside.

"What museum did you raid?" Boss smirked.

Dee gave Boss an over-the-glasses librarian look. She waited for a cheeky response, but he just looked at his feet and kept silent. Satisfied that Boss knew it was serious, Dee glanced at the others gathered round.

"So, we need to decide what to do. Do we continue scrounging through houses for food? Or do we make a run for it? Get somewhere more isolated? Fewer Variants?"

Dee pressed on. "If we stay, we just keep scavenging in ever-increasing circles, hoping for food. We could try a food wholesalers. And we need guns desperately. Or, and this is what I vote for, we take my car and try to reach this valley," she said, pointing at the map. "Jack and I have a cabin there."

"Well, I vote to stay. Surely the army is going to show up soon," Mike said, "and take us to one of those evac centres."

"What army?" Matt asked. "New Zealand doesn't have an army."

"Yeah, we do!" Mike replied, his voice rising.

"Guys! Seriously," Alice said. "Matt, give it a rest. And Mike, he's teasing you."

Dee flicked her eyes between them. After ten days of hiding, everyone was getting on each other's nerves. She knew they had to move on. It was time.

"Yes we do have an army," Aston cut in, nodding. "It's small, but it's there. Regardless, they're not worried about rescuing us mere mortals. We're on our own."

There were murmurs of agreement.

"I ran into a couple of soldiers out there," Dee said. Boss looked at her, eyes wide. He had asked her about how she'd survived, but she'd skirted the subject, not wanting to dampen his spirits. "I don't think they're going to be much help."

Alice turned to Matt and poked him. "We should tell them."

"Tell us what?" asked Dee.

"Yeah, what?" mimicked Boss.

Matt, Alice and Aston exchanged a look between them. Matt sighed and looked down at the maps.

"Look, we want to head off on our own," he said. "Alice's family owns a sheep station on one of the islands in the Gulf. We're going to head there. Plus, I want to find my family."

"Dee, we're really grateful, truly, but I need to know. Know if they're alive," Alice said, looking at Dee.

"I can't argue with that, Alice. I only have Jack. That's why I want to go to the cabin." She clasped Alice's hand. "I really hope they're okay."

The two women smiled at each other, hope, anguish and worry for their loved ones written deep in their eyes.

Dee had only known Alice for few days, but she wished it had been in different circumstances. Over the years she'd found it difficult to stay in contact with her friends as they all got married and had children.

"Take the back roads. Last I heard, the motorway was jammed," Dee said.

Alice and Matt nodded.

"Well, that's just crazy. Safety in numbers, anyone?" Mike said, slamming his fist on the table.

Vicki glared at Mike. "Shush, for Pete's sake."

Dee glared at him too. Days of putting up with his foul moods and impudence finally got the better of her. "All they want is to see their families. You want to deny them that?" Speaking through her teeth, Dee added, "Or is it the lack of an invite?"

Mike started gesturing madly, his face going red. He started to retort, but Vicki elbowed him in the ribs,

116

effectively silencing him.

"We're happy to go with you, Dee. Our families are both in the South Island. Just until it blows over, then we'll be on our way," Vicki whispered. She bent down next to Dee. "I'm sorry about Mike."

Dee shrugged her shoulders and grimaced. "I don't know about you lot, but I've had enough of this basement and its foul stench." She looked at Boss, causing him to grin, and once again she marvelled at the teenager's resilience. Seeing his smile gave her new motivation.

"Matt?"

"Yeah?"

"You can take my neighbour's car. I know where the keys are."

Matt nodded. "That sounds perfect. Thank you."

The group spent the next hour gathering what little food and water they had, dividing it up as evenly as they could. Dee gave them all spare clothes from some bags she had meant to take to the op shop.

Picking up her katana, Dee looked at Boss still trying to cram all the radio bits into a box. "C'mon, they'll be active again soon."

"Yeah I know, I just don't want to miss anything."

"Okay. Meet us in the car. And be careful."

Distracted, Boss nodded.

Matt was waiting at the basement door, and as Dee approached, he looked over at Aston, who was peering through the grate. Given the all clear, Matt slid the bolt and they stepped out into the sunlight.

Dee took a deep breath, the fresh air filling her lungs. Looking left and right, she gripped the katana tightly.

Seeing nothing, she walked on. Dread washed over her the closer she got to her elderly neighbour's house. The thought of seeing Faye's mangled body frightened Dee, but she knew she had to do this. She wanted to survive, to see Jack again.

I didn't fight the darkness for it to end now.

Dee walked up to the smashed-in window and quickly peered inside. On the floor was a thick, congealed blood stain, but no body. She frowned. *Where's the body?* Matt brushed against her as he looked in too.

Not wanting to speak for fear of attracting Variants, Dee, using mime, demonstrated that she wanted Matt to cup his hands together and give her a boost.

Grunting, Matt pushed her through the window and onto the kitchen bench. Dee did her best to stay out of the glass, but she felt a few pinpricks on her hands. Looking again to the spot where the body had lain, shivers shot up her spine. Quickly moving on, she grabbed the keys off the hook near the pantry and let herself out the side door.

Signalling with a nod of her head, she indicated the garage to Matt and handed him the keys.

They were struggling with the garage door as Aston and Alice joined them.

"Wait a few minutes. We'll try to leave together," Dee said, lowering her voice.

Matt nodded.

Alice grabbed Dee in a bear hug. "Thank you."

Pushing Alice back slightly, Dee wiped a tear from her own eye. "You're welcome. Good luck, and thanks for all the fish."

Alice smiled distantly at her, not getting the reference.

Embarrassed, Dee jumped over the fence. Crouching low, she made a dash for her car. When she got to her garage, she found Mike and Boss had raised the garage door in readiness. They piled into the car and she turned the ignition. Easing the car out, she glanced around, looking for Variants. Gripping the steering wheel, she indicated right and headed up the road, away from her sanctuary. Dee wondered if she was doing the right thing by leaving. Would Jack know to head to the cabin? She pushed her doubts aside and concentrated on driving everyone to safety.

Matt followed her to the end of the road. Turning south, Dee and her group waved them goodbye. She watched as their car disappeared from view and said a silent prayer of hope. Hope that they would survive to see their families again.

— 17 —

Dee made it across town without incident, weaving in and out of the vehicles that clogged the road. Everywhere they looked there was evidence of violent confrontations. Blood and broken glass. She saw one car with the doors peeled off like a tin of sardines.

What the hell did that?

Dee drove them to a hunting shop she knew, but they could see it had been looted. Giving up on finding any new guns, they drove on, heading for one of the bridges crossing the river. As they drew near, she could see it was blocked. Vehicles were strewn everywhere, tangled in a bottleneck. Some were burnt out.

"We'll have to try the next bridge down," Dee said.

"They'll all be the same," Mike said sullenly.

Dee shook her head in annoyance. "We have to try though."

"What about Narrows Bridge, out by the airport?" asked Boss.

"Yeah, all right. Less traffic. Could be a winner," agreed Dee.

Reversing the car, Dee looked in the rearview mirror,

and mouthed *Thank you* to Boss.

The going was slow, as all the roads were nearly impassable. She had to backtrack several times and try different routes, but finally they made it out of Hamilton. Speeding up as much as she dared, Dee couldn't help thinking that the Variants would be out on the hunt in another couple of hours.

If the roads carry on like this, we're going to have to find somewhere to hole up for the night.

The Narrows Golf Course shimmered into view as Dee swerved around another abandoned vehicle. She slowed, knowing the bridge was just around the corner, and crossed her fingers for some luck. Her heart sank. Just like the others, the bridge was clogged.

Damn it!

Several cars were pressed against each other, like a police roadblock. Looking into the jumbled mess, she could see a small gap, perhaps just wide enough to squeeze the car through.

"What do you think, guys?"

"We could shunt them over a bit," Mike said. "Do you want me to drive?"

"I got it."

"Are you sure?"

Dee glared at Matt. "Yes. Just keep an eye on your side."

"Fine. I was only offering."

Dee let out a breath to calm her anger and inched the car forwards, scraping both fenders. The metallic sound echoed around the car. She clenched her jaw and pressed the accelerator down, giving the car more gas.

Easy, easy does it.

Dee checked the wing mirrors in turn, checking her progress. She heard the thump a fraction before Vicki and Mike screamed. Looking up, she saw a Variant perched on the roof of a nearby car. It stared at them with its reptilian yellow eyes. Globs of saliva drooled from its mouth.

Dee felt her heart drop like she was on a rollercoaster. She grabbed the gear stick, jammed the car into reverse and slammed the accelerator down, spinning the tyres.

The Variant shrieked and leapt onto the hood of her car. Several screeches answered its call. Dee swung the steering wheel hard from side to side, trying to remove the Variant, but it dug its claw-like digits into the hood.

One arm drew back and smashed through the windscreen, spearing a stunned Mike right through the skull. Vicki's screams jumped several octaves.

Boss pounded Dee's shoulder. "Down there! Go right, through the golf course!"

She didn't have time to answer. Swinging the steering wheel hard right, the car whipped back and went down the embankment. They rolled once before righting and, wheels spinning in the soft earth, Dee put it into drive and tore away from the screeching Variants.

The roll had crushed the Variant that had speared Mike, whose lifeless body flopped around and leaned onto Dee.

"Boss, get him off me!" she shouted.

Boss pushed Mike against the passenger door with his feet.

Dee kept the accelerator pressed against the floor, the car fish-tailing over the grass like they were competing in a rally. She dodged trees and shrubs and even one overturned golf cart with clubs scattered next to it.

Tearing over the pristine greens, she looked around frantically for an escape route.

"Over there!" Boss shouted, pointing to a large motorboat moored at a pier. "Let's see if these bastards can swim."

Dee turned her head in the direction he was pointing and nodded. She spun the wheel and swung the car towards the boat. As she checked in the rearview mirror, she spotted dozens more Variants joining the hunt. Some ran on all fours while others ran upright, more human-like. Others still bounced along, shrieking. The car left the ground and Dee gasped as it smashed into a sand trap. Her chest slammed into the steering wheel, the air whooshing out of her lungs. Grunting with pain, she looked back at the Variants. She was stunned at their speed and agility.

"Run," Dee gasped. Boss tossed her pack, the katana strapped to the webbing. She caught it and they sprinted for the boat.

"Hurry."

The Variants screeched in unison as they ran. Dee stole a glance back to check if Boss and Vicki were following.

Over the crest of the hill, several Variants were moving towards them, fast. She slowed, letting Boss pass her.

Reaching the boat, Boss scrambled to start the engine. "Get in," he shouted. His eyes went wide. "Vicki! No!"

Dee spun and searched out the other woman. Vicki stood at the end of the jetty, arms outstretched like Christ the Redeemer. She turned her head back towards Dee and looked into her eyes. And in that moment, Dee saw Vicki's anguish over Mike's death. She had given up. This was her sacrifice. Her heaven-entering deed. For them to survive. To live on.

Dee looked in horror as the leading Variants slammed into Vicki, tearing and fighting over her flesh.

"Dee! Come on!" Boss screamed.

Scrambling and slipping on the jetty, she covered the last few metres and with a swish of her katana, cut the bowline and jumped in.

Boss gunned the engine and the boat surged out into the river.

A lone Variant bolted from the pack. With an awe-inspiring leap, it sailed through the air towards the fleeing survivors.

Dee pivoted and, with all the anger and frustration that had eaten away at her for the past fifteen days being cooped up in that stinking basement, she let out a screaming war cry, bringing her katana up in a slashing arc.

The Variant twisted in mid-air in an attempt to avoid the swinging steel, but Dee's blow cut deep into its torso, nearly severing it in two. With a sickening thud, it landed quivering in a heap on the boat deck.

Disgusted, Dee kicked it into the river.

Boss stared at her. "You're getting good with that."

Dee shrugged her shoulders and looked back to the river bank where the other Variants had gathered in a pack, screeching. They were jumping up and down but did not enter the water. She could see more of them on the bridge.

"Looks like we can only go that way, upriver towards

Cambridge," Dee said pointing to the town south of Hamilton.

Boss nodded in agreement. "Okay."

Dee sat down in the seat next to him as he moved the boat into the current and away from the beasts. Taking a moment to calm herself, she looked around the largish boat and saw that it was kitted out for pleasure cruising. *Huh? What people spend their money on.* She shook her head.

Boss looked over at her, a frown creasing his forehead. "You know what, Dee?"

"What Boss?"

"You're not what I was expecting."

"Well, as they say, you have to expect the unexpected."

"Who's they?"

Even amongst all the horror they had witnessed over the past couple of weeks, Dee found herself smiling at Boss, shaking her head in amusement.

Where are you, Jack?

— 18 —

The primal screech echoed through the warm damp air, reverberating off the walls and jolting Jack from his fitful sleep. He snapped his eyes open and looked left and right, heart hammering. Trying to calm himself, he forced his breathing to slow. Listening for the tell-tale popping sounds the creatures made, Jack took note of his surroundings.

He was in a corridor, its floors and walls made of concrete. Twisting his head as far he could, it seemed to go on forever in both directions. A constant humming buzzed in his ears, like someone had left an engine running. Surrounding him, other people were glued to the walls in the same way he was, behind a white cocoon or some such thing. No one moved, and given the stench of death, some appeared to be long dead. It reminded Jack of a science fiction film he had seen in his youth; the title escaped him. He remembered the victims being used as incubators.

Is that what I am? An incubator?

His fevered mind struggled to grasp what he was seeing. He had no idea how long he'd been down here. His throbbing head and intense hunger told him it was several days, at least.

Jack could feel the tube of his water bladder resting on his left shoulder. Fleeting memories of the last few days returned, flashing in his mind's eye.

Struggling against his bonds; rubbing his wrist raw; water so tantalizingly close. Screeching. Clacking. Cutting. Thud...!

With all his remaining strength, he pushed his butt against the wall, relieving some of the pressure on his right arm, which was twisted uncomfortably so the back of his hand touched the concrete wall, the membrane holding it fast. This time, he managed to wrench his left arm free. He grabbed the water valve and, twisting it towards his mouth, sucked on the tube, releasing the tepid but wonderful water into his mouth. Jack could feel it as it ran all the way down to his rumbling stomach. Gulping a few mouthfuls, he stopped himself from drinking too much. Making himself sick would attract his captors.

His mind began to clear. Pushing his left arm back under the membrane, he felt along the waist belt of his hiking pack for the little pouch. Finding it, he unzipped it. Slowly, fearful of alerting the monsters, he removed one of his protein bars. Rabidly he tore off the wrapper. Forgetting about the creatures, he fed his hunger. To survive, he had to eat.

With his appetite sated and his thirst quenched, Jack took stock of his situation.

What is it that guy always said? There's always a way out?

All right. I'm stuck to a wall. In some horror-filled nightmare. Surrounded by dead or dying people. Creatures from the seventh circle of hell want to eat me.

Great. Just great.

Typical.

Jack tore at the membrane holding his right arm fast against the wall, stopping every few seconds to listen. Hell, but the stuff was tough. Again and again he pulled on it. It was like trying to tear a plastic shopping bag at the handles: it stretched but refused to break. With a final tug, he managed to free his right arm.

The stench of rotten fruit wafted down the corridor, alerting him to creatures approaching. Clenching all his muscles tight, he rammed his arms back into position and went stiff as a board.

They scurried along the corridor, their joints popping as they moved. Jack risked a peek through his semi-closed eyelids as his heart pounded harder against his chest. Two of the beasts had stopped a few metres away and were sniffing the human stuck to the wall in front of them. Jack couldn't help but look. Scared as he was at being discovered, his natural curiosity begged him to observe these strange creatures.

Perhaps if I learn their routines, I can find a weakness.

One of the creatures used its claw-like appendages to quickly saw through a membrane, and as he watched, a blonde-haired woman dropped to the floor with a thud. Jack flinched at the sound of her body hitting the concrete. The other monster bent down. Its tongue flicked out and licked the woman's face. The monster scooped her up with ease and flung her over its shoulder. It made a weird clicking sound to the other beast before the pair turned and scurried away.

Jack was about to look away when a shadow to one side caught his attention.

A short, overweight man with a red trucker's cap

loomed into the light. He scratched his butt and looked over towards Jack. He spat on the floor next to a red-haired woman and reached up and groped her breasts.

"Pity. This one's pretty," Trucker-cap said, his voice bouncing off the walls.

He kissed the woman and shuffled off after the creatures.

A man was walking around in this place of horrors, unscathed?

Jack's foggy mind struggled to comprehend it. He inhaled to call out to him for help, but some innate sense stopped him. He just stared as the man walked away down the corridor. The whole thing felt wrong to Jack. Very, very wrong. He wanted answers. Needed answers.

Where am I?

How long have I been here?

What is this place?

Why is that creep walking around when the rest of us are stuck to the walls?

With renewed determination, Jack redoubled his efforts to get free. He wanted to see Dee again. To see those beautiful, smiling eyes. To feel her reassuring touch. He needed her. When Dee was around, everything seemed right.

He wondered what was happening to her. She must surely be really worried about him by now.

With both arms now free, he started working on liberating his legs. Pulling, tearing, twisting. Jack tried biting it with his teeth but the membrane tasted foul, like rotten lemons. It burned his lips and the roof of his mouth. He tried to ignore the taste but the more he bit into it, the more it burned.

Finally, he got one leg free and was able to twist his

body. With one last shove, Jack wrenched the rest of his body free and landed on the floor with a thud. Cringing, he glanced down the corridor in the direction the creatures had gone, followed by Trucker-cap. Seeing nothing and, more importantly, hearing nothing, he gingerly got to his feet. As soon as he put weight on his right leg, he winced in pain. He quickly adjusted his weight off the leg. A blood-stained bandage was wrapped around it. Removing the bandage, Jack found a gash that ran twenty centimetres up his thigh from his knee, cutting deep into the skin. Congealed blood had crusted around the wound but plasma was beginning to seep, thanks to his recent activity.

Jack looked left and right before quietly removing his pack. He opened the bottom compartment, pulling out the outdoorman's best friend: a roll of duct tape. Tearing off a segment, he closed the wound as best he could and wrapped the bandage back around his leg. Happy with his field dressing, he tested his weight on the injured leg. It still throbbed, but with the new strapping it felt marginally better.

Time to leave.

Warm air flowed over him as he made his way down the long corridor. With no other plan coming to mind, Jack had decided to head towards the humming sound. Treading carefully down the centre of the corridor, he kept his focus straight ahead. He dared not look to either side, at the other victims strung up like slaughtered cattle. Waiting to be butchered and fed upon.

Jack didn't want to put any faces into his memory, traumatised as it was. *What if he saw someone he knew? Could he deal with that? What if he saw Dee?* This last thought made him pause and crouch down. Forcing himself to breathe slow and deep, Jack looked farther down the corridor. About halfway down was a door with a big red sign on it, but the text was unintelligible. With something to focus on, he was about to rise when something moved at the edge of his vision. Half stumbling, he fell back on his arse. Staring into his eyes was a young red-haired boy, his ice blue eyes piercing. Jack knew him, and as he stared back, his tired, traumatised mind cleared.

Shivering in the river, half floating, half swimming, Jack could see the creatures on the banks. There seemed to be packs of them. Never entering the water. They weren't afraid, just unsure…

Following him, they gathered into larger packs. Screeching. Howling. Spitting.

Occasionally their heads would lift, sniffing the air, and they would tear off with excited howls, gone for a time. Jack enjoyed these interludes. He didn't feel so on edge, waiting for one of them to pluck up the courage and dive in for him. But they returned…always. And in greater numbers.

He laughed to himself; they were like the sandpeople! If Dee was here, she would be telling Jack to be serious, but this was his superpower. His coping mechanism. Always finding the silly side of something, or finding a movie or TV reference in anything. He had once been on the wrong side of an armed robbery and had had a gun pointed at his head. This was how he'd got through the trauma.

He remembered meeting Emma, the two of them floating down the river and onto Lake Arapuni. Their search for a boat, the run in with Duke and his men. His escape.

Finding Sarah and George in the school. Cambridge and the evac centre. Rescuing Emma. The creatures ambushing them. The big leader and the darkness.

Jack remembered it all.

Right in front of him, the same boy held out his arm to Jack, his ice blue eyes pleading. Jack shook his head. Fate was strange. Rising to his knees, he remembered he had a little Swiss Army Knife in his first aid kit. Praying the creatures wouldn't hear him, he searched his pack, hurrying. Pulling out the knife, he made quick work of the strange muck holding George to the wall.

George collapsed into his arms, whimpering. He eased the boy down to the ground and gave him the water valve. Seeing the liquid move along the tube, he searched around for Sarah.

Jack jogged a few metres up the corridor, now looking at each face. Searching. Blonde hair? No. Move on. He saw kids, adults, elderly, Maori, European, Asian, Pacific. It really didn't matter. Everyone was here. The population. Food. Not seeing Sarah, Jack knew he and George needed to keep moving. Lingering any longer increased risk of discovery.

— 19 —

Jack lifted George into his arms and made his way towards the door with the red sign, continuing to search faces as he went. Not seeing Sarah, he hurried on, eager to get out of sight. Eager to eat something. Eager to leave this cursed place.

He could see the sign on the door now: SWITCH ROOM. The walls on either side looked new, with fresh green paint.

Jack tried the handle. Grinning as it turned, he hurried through. As he put George down, the boy whimpered. He crouched down till he was at eye level. George stared at him vacantly. In that fleeting moment, he realised all the horror the poor kid had seen in the last few days. Grasping his shoulder, Jack comforted him.

"You're safe now, George."

George blinked his eyes rapidly but remained silent.

Jack frowned and let out a breath as he took in the layout of the large room. On either side of the door were storage lockers. On the left- and right-hand walls stood rows of metal cupboards. In the far-right corner were more storage lockers. A small hand basin stood in the far-left corner, while a small window was set centrally in the wall opposite. Bright sunlight shone onto the floor of the room. Opening one of the cupboards revealed panels of switches similar to those on a household meter board, but industrial-scale. Jack read the labels: UTILITY ROOM; TURBINE ROOM; GATE HOUSE and smiled. He knew what these were. They controlled power to the various rooms of whatever building he was in. Jack scanned the labels again. Turbine Room stood out. You normally only found turbines in power stations.

Moving to the small window set in the opposite wall, he looked out. Below him surged a river.

And then all the clues added up. The switch labels, the north-facing dam, the large river below it… The mighty Waikato River.

And we're in the bloody dam! They're imprisoning us in the dam! Why?

Jack gazed out the window, hoping for further clues as to which hydro-electric dam they were in.

"Mum?" croaked George.

"What's up buddy?" Jack said, hurrying over.

"I want my mum."

Jack paused. *Do I tell him the truth? Sugarcoat it?* He went for in between.

"Still out there, buddy. You and I are going to be like Spiderman and save her. What do you think of that?"

George nodded in agreement, his eyes cast to the floor.

"You must be hungry, eh?" Jack said, lifting George's chin up and wiping away his tears.

"Yup," George whispered.

"Okay buddy, you hang in there. I just want to

barricade this door first, okay?"

Jack quickly searched the room for anything to lean up against the door. He didn't want to drag anything across the floor, so the lockers were out.

He moved past the metal switch cupboards to the back of the room where the storage lockers were. They were set against adjacent walls and a gap had been left in the corner. It was perfect. It wouldn't help against any monsters, but it might be of use if the fat guy came along.

Collecting George, he hoisted him up to sit on top of the lockers, then hauled himself up and down the other side and lifted George down. Pulling all his clothes out of his pack, he made them into a sort of bean bag to sit on. Jack opened his snack box.

"Chocolate?"

The little red-head kid smiled at him as he handed him a bar of Whittaker's. They ate in silence, enjoying the sweet treat.

Jack looked down at George eating and thought about the other boy he'd tried to save. The creatures had attacked them so fast he'd had no time to save Flatcap and his family. Jack pushed the image of the little boy being torn apart from his mind. Now was not the time to dwell on it. He glanced at George again. Chocolate smeared around his face.

Jack reached out and ruffled his hair, grinning at the little fighter. "Well, George, how do we get out of the Pit of Despair?"

George shrugged his shoulders, rested his head against Jack's chest and fell asleep.

Jack stared out the window a long time, turning everything over in his mind. He ran through a thousand scenarios trying to figure a way to escape, but kept drawing a blank.

Finally, he let sleep take him.

— 20 —

Dee stirred in the bottom of the boat and stretched out her cramped legs. She could see Boss hunched over the steering wheel. Focused on keeping the boat in the middle of the river.

The pack of Variants had tracked them upriver all night, screeching at them. Howling at them. Dee had watched them for hours, cringing inwardly every time they uttered a sound. It was a noise that no matter how many times you heard it, it never got easier to bear.

Dee was surprised she had fallen asleep. Her nerves were a tattered mess. Searching the river banks, there was no sign of the monsters now. She glanced up at the sky, thankful for the sunshine. It gave them a chance to move on land.

"Hey." She smiled, looking at Boss.

"Hey." Boss turned and yawned. "About time you woke up."

"Why didn't you wake me. I would've taken the wheel."

"You looked exhausted."

"Any idea where we are?" Dee said, standing.

"Still out in farming land, by the smell. Variants buggered off about an hour ago."

"About time. Don't know if I could've handled that much longer. I felt like a goldfish being watched by a ravenous cat."

"What do you mean? You slept all night."

"Well, someone had to." Dee smiled. She scanned around, searching. "C'mon. Let's find some food. And we really need a gun. Farmers are good for guns, right?"

"Yeah, I suppose." Boss shrugged and yawned again.

He spun the wheel and moved the boat closer towards the shore. Dee stood next to him and gripped her katana as she searched the bank for Variants, fearful of them darting out of the shadows. Swarming the boat and tearing them apart. They waited in the boat with the engine switched off. Dee could hear birds and insects and the rustle of trees in the late morning breeze but everything else remained silent. Satisfied, she tapped Boss on the shoulder and leapt from the boat.

"Let's go. Silently," Dee whispered.

Dee and Boss kept to the tree line. Creeping along, they tracked inland, making for one of the houses. It was a single-storey brick home with a large deck extending from the back. A couple of large sheds lay adjacent. Keeping to the shadows of the trees, Dee and Boss cautiously came up one side. They stopped a few metres from the back door. Heart pounding, Dee gripped the katana for comfort. She looked for any signs of occupants, or Variants. Glancing left and right, she came up clear. Not a sound came from the house.

"What do you think?" Dee said, nudging Boss.

"I don't know?" Boss said, shrugging.

Dee forced herself to remain calm. She wasn't used to dealing with a teenager's attitude. She let out a breath. "Boss, I'm sorry you didn't get any sleep last night, all right? But right now we need to focus on getting some food, and hopefully a gun or two. Something to better fight the Variants with. So let's just do this, then get back to the boat. You can get some sleep then, okay?"

"Okay, sure, cool, whatever. But we need petrol too."

Dee waited for Boss to add anything else. When he didn't, she rose up and headed for the back door.

As Dee approached the door, she could see it was open a crack. Frowning, her heart skipped a beat. She peered in through the gap. No movement. No tell-tale rotten fruit smell. Looking back at Boss, she raised a finger to her lips.

Dee pushed the door open wider with the tip of her katana. Inside, she could see the kitchen. Drawers had been pulled out, cupboards opened and emptied. Ransacked. It looked like the only food left was dried pasta and rice.

Dee and Boss slowly made their way through the kitchen and into the living area of the house. Arriving at the bedrooms, she could see that whoever had lived here had made a hasty retreat. Unpacked clothes lay on the beds, along with personal items too big to fit in suitcases.

Damn! I wonder if they have any guns?

Boss moved to the wardrobes, rummaging through them. "Hey, Dee, these would be handy." He held out two fleece zip-up jackets.

"Definitely, nice find. Keep looking. I'm going to hunt for food, okay?"

"Yeah, all right. What else should we grab?"

"See if you can find a couple of backpacks."

Dee headed into the other rooms, searching. Coming up empty-handed, she went back to Boss searching around in the master bedroom.

"Find anything else?"

"Nah," Boss said.

Dee ran her hands through her hair and sighed. "All right. Let's try that other house we saw. I think we should hurry though."

"We should grab that rice and pasta, at least," Boss murmured. "And what about guns?"

"I figure the family living here took them when they cleared out."

"We should at least check the garage. Or those sheds," Boss said. "We need petrol for the boat."

"Okay." Dee nodded.

The sheds had the usual open fronts. Dee could see a couple of big farm machines taking up most of the space. She had no idea what they did. With all the prongs and blades poking out, they looked like some medieval torture devices. She sighed. If Jack was here he'd be telling her about some horror movie he'd watched. Even acting out a scene where the machines had been used to kill someone.

"Dee? You okay?" Boss said, frowning at her.

Dee blinked away her thoughts of Jack and looked around the sheds. "Fine."

"What about in there?" Boss said, pointing at a white metal cabinet in the far back corner. It had dirt encrusted tarps stacked on top of it and several containers of nauseating liquid piled beside it. Some of the container lids were lying scattered on the floor. Dee shook her head at the mess.

"Yes. It's a possibility."

Dee hurried over. Deep gouges and scratches on the doors became visible as she drew nearer, and the heavy padlock had been cut and tossed aside. Someone had beaten them to it again.

Dee growled inwardly and clenched her hands into fists. She was frustrated, hungry and tired. All she wanted was to find Jack and get to the cabin. When he hadn't shown up back at the house for over ten days, she had assumed the worst. Only determination and her love for Jack had kept her going. She could feel the weight falling off her from the lack of food and the now-constant fear of the creatures. Creatures from some sick nightmare. Variants, Boss called them. Dee wondered, for the hundredth time, *Variants of what?*

Dee felt a slight breeze on her neck, she pivoted and gasped. A shotgun was pointing straight at her. Another was at Boss's head. Two tall, overweight men held them. Dee looked down the barrel and into the hard brown eyes of her captor, who was grinning at her, missing front teeth. Dee cursed herself. She'd been so caught up in her thoughts she hadn't heard the men approach.

Missing Teeth winked at her. "Hello, sweetcheeks. You looking for these?" He waggled the gun.

"Yeah, we were, actually. Want to give them to us?" Dee glared back as she inched her hand towards her katana strapped to her back.

"Naughty. Naughty," Missing Teeth said. "Hands where I can see them."

Dee held up her hands. "What do you want?"

"You, of course."

"I don't think so," Dee said. She breathed deeply and stepped closer to the smelly chemicals.

"You're funny. And cute too. This is going to be fun." With his gun, he gestured towards a wooden pallet. "Go sit over there. If you seem like you're enjoying it, I'll put a good word in with the monsters."

The reality of the situation dawned on her. Rape. Even at the end of the bloody world, these bastards just wanted to live out their sick fantasies. Typical.

"Guys, c'mon please. It should be us against the Variants. Not this!" Dee said. She held out her hands palms down, trying to pacify the situation.

"Variants?"

"Yes, Variants. The Americans call them Variants."

Missing Teeth stared at her. He frowned and his face reddened. Dee thought she saw a hint of confusion flit across his eyes before he spat on the floor.

"Look, sweetcheeks, I don't give a toss what some Yankee Doodle Dandy called them. Simon and I are going to have a little fun with you. SO MOVE YOUR ARSE, NOW!"

Missing Teeth grabbed Dee by her shirt front and hauled her to her feet. Dee started screaming as loud as she could. Struggling against the man's grip, she kicked out at his shins.

"It'll do you no good. It's just us. Soon you'll be with our monster friends. So kick and scream all you want."

Boss started struggling with Simon, trying to wrestle the gun away from him, but Simon was too strong, too quick. He leant back and swung the gun stock, connecting with Boss's head in a savage blow. Boss hit the ground like a sack of potatoes.

Dee watched him thud to the ground. "He's just a kid, you bastards!" she screamed at the men.

Missing Teeth and Simon laughed as they dragged her over to a wooden pallet covered with wool sacks. They started whooping and hollering like a couple of boozed-up teenagers.

Dee fought with everything she had. There was no way they were going to take her. She had fought off guys before. She blamed the rape culture for the way men thought they were entitled to act. In a flash, a memory raced through her mind.

A water-filled quarry. Dee and her friends were enjoying the last of the summer before university. A few drinks in the sun. She fell asleep under a tree while her friends swam out to the rock in the middle of the lake.

Dee woke to a rough, calloused hand over her mouth and hands grabbing roughly at her. She struggled and fought like a trapped cat. Finally, she connected with a well-timed knee to the groin. The man tumbled off her, clutching his balls. He rolled around on the ground, cursing at her. A red mist descended over her. She picked up a nearby rock and smashed the man in the head. Again and again and again. Another man Dee hadn't seen tackled her, knocking her to the ground and out of her rage. Seeing her friends running up from the lake shore, the second man ran off. Dee looked down at the rock she still held. She could see blood and grey brain matter, and tiny fragments of skull. She promptly doubled over and vomited.

The police arrived and took Dee away in an ambulance. Later they arrested her for manslaughter.

A lengthy emotional and soul-destroying trial ensued. It exposed Dee to a very corrupt and male-favoured system. Psychiatric evaluations deemed her fit for trial, but thankfully she was found not guilty by means of self-defence. The media called her the mouse that roared. The rapist's family yelled daily abuse at her. After that, she withdrew from society, finding comfort in books. In movies. In gaming. Where people are essentially anonymous.

It took meeting a special guy to bring her out of her shell. To live life on the outside again.

Dee would always remember the stench of her attacker's breath. A mixture of cheap bourbon and cannabis.

— 21 —

Thinking of her past gave Dee strength. She reached down inside herself and began to struggle as if her life depended on it. She scratched. She kicked. She ripped her fingernails over Missing Teeth's face and bit into his hand.

"Hmmm... I like it when they fight." He grinned down at her. "Hold the bitch's legs down."

Simon grabbed both her flailing legs in a vice-like grip. Together, the men managed to wrestle her onto the pallet.

She looked up into Missing Teeth's eyes, silently pleading with him. Searching for some decency. Hoping to change his mind while looking into his eyes. Hoping to ease the evil in his soul. Anything to stop what was about to happen.

Dee didn't hear the first gunshot. Missing Teeth's head exploded, brains and skull splattering all over her. The sight of his lust-filled eyes seared into her memory. His body slumped, pinning her legs.

She heard the next couple of shots and saw Simon look down at the gaping holes in his chest. His lifeless body toppled over. Dee shuddered and pushed Missing Teeth's body off her. She stood and stared down at his nearly headless body and she spat on him.

Asshole.

"You all right?"

Dee spun towards the source of the voice. A stocky, muscular man with a long wizard beard and white hair approached her. He was dressed in green cargo pants, a green shirt and a black combat vest filled with magazines and even a grenade or two.

"You all right?" he asked again.

"Y...Yeah, I think so." Dee shook her head. Too many things were happening at once today. "Boss?"

"Sorry, what?"

"Boss. Sorry, I mean the kid?"

"He'll be fine. He took a nasty blow to the head, though."

"Thank you," Dee said, kicking Missing Teeth again. "I'm Dee. I call the kid Boss."

"You're welcome. Ben. Ben Johns." He glanced around, eyes alert. "We need to move, I don't know how many of those creatures have been alerted by the gunshots."

"At this time of day?"

"Yes," Ben said. "Let's grab the kid and go."

"We've got a boat tied up down at the river. The Variants won't come in the water."

"Variants? You call them Variants too, huh?" A bemused look crossed Ben's face.

Dee's head snapped up at the distant sound of shrieks.

"Umm, yeah, ah. Boss had an old ham radio going and he talked to some Americans. They called them Variants."

"Right. Well, the Variants, they are smart bastards, and fast. Why don't you come back to my bunker? I've got food, water and medical supplies. It's held them out for now."

She searched Ben's eyes and found honesty and kindness. She nodded, more to herself than to him. "All right, thank you."

Ben and Dee grabbed an arm each and hauled Boss to his feet. He was coming to, but was still groggy. Ben led them to a 4x4 parked next to a red ute, his eyes constantly flicking around.

Dee could hear more shrieks but the Variants remained distant for now. If Ben felt any panic, he didn't show it. Dee observed the way he moved. Fluid. Alert. Completely aware of his surroundings. Like he knew where everything was located. Exit points. Everything.

They pushed Boss onto the back seat and laid him down. Dee grabbed one of the fleece jackets they'd found and placed it under his head.

Ben eased them out of the farm driveway and onto the sealed road. He pointed the 4x4 east and picked up speed.

"Here, use these to clean some of that muck off you." Ben handed Dee some tissues.

"Thanks."

"I'm not far. About fifteen minutes."

She nodded. She couldn't figure it out. Why had Ben been there? She was more than grateful, of course. She looked down at the rifle sitting between them. It was black, but had a long, fat, extended barrel. It looked military. Not like the ones her dad used to use. Ben looked and acted like military. With shooting like that and the calm way he acted, she guessed he was ex-army.

"So. Look, thanks for saving us back there."

"You're welcome. I couldn't stand by and let them do that. It's not right. Even in these terrifying times, there are rules. Moral rules." Ben glanced over, smiled, and stroked his long bushy beard.

Dee could see by the expression on the old man's face that he was telling the truth. She decided she liked him already. Plus, he seemed really handy with a rifle. If she wanted any chance of finding Jack, she needed Ben. His expertise.

Till now she'd been extremely lucky, but luck will only get you so far. She knew she reacted well under pressure. A calmness would come over her as if time slowed down and she saw the way out. More than anything, she wanted to survive this. She wanted Jack back. To take them all to the valley, to start afresh.

"Ben?" Dee said, picking and brushing the last of the skull fragments off her chest and arms and trying not to gag.

"Yeah?"

"I'm curious. How did you know we were there?"

"I didn't. But I knew they were. I'd been tracking their movements for a few days."

Dee looked at Ben, startled. *Tracking them? For a few days? Why?* She opened her mouth to ask, but Ben slowed the 4x4 down and turned onto a tree-lined driveway, magnolia trees creating an avenue.

"We're here," he announced.

Dee looked down the drive and could see it curving up behind a small hill. As the 4x4 got closer to the hill, a house nestled into the leeward side came into view. It looked as though the walls were made of earth and she could barely make out the roof line. Wildflowers covered it.

Ben pulled up around the back, next to a large utility shed. This too blended into the surrounding countryside.

Ben and Dee half-dragged a semi-conscious Boss out of the 4x4. Ben indicated with a tilt of his head towards a side door. Entering the house, it struck Dee how warm and dry it was. And with the door closed behind them, the silence was complete.

Jack would love this house. It looked like a safe place, retreating a good ten metres or so into the hill.

Ben guided her and Boss past some shelves towards a couple of bunks in the back left-hand corner of the room. Dee struggled with the deadweight that was Boss. Pain shot up her arms and the muscles in her lower back started to cramp. She concentrated on putting one foot in front of the other, watching the smooth concrete floor as sweat dripped off her forehead from the exertion. Once there, they gently laid Boss down.

"First aid and medical supplies are in here." Ben pointed to a large medical cabinet on the wall. "I'm heading outside to lock up and set the sensors."

"Thanks Ben," Dee said. "Oh hey, do you have any fertiliser? We used to use it to mask our scent."

Ben picked up a large twenty-litre container, grinning. His sharp eyes appraised her. "Not just a pretty face, are you? I use this. Industrial grade disinfectant. I'll be back."

Dee watched him go. Normally she would be offended by such a remark, but Ben was an up-front guy. A spade was a spade. She busied herself cleaning out the wound on Boss's head.

Boss tried to get up, tried to speak. Dee helped him

swallow a couple of painkillers and pushed him back down. "Sleep, Boss."

She heard Ben come back into the room and the huge steel door shut with a clunk. Dee got up and walked over to him. He slid thick bolts across the door, locking them in. Happy that they were secure, Dee turned and took in her new surroundings. She was impressed to see block walls all around. The concrete floor she had already noted. To the left and right were shelves filled with food, water and plastic containers. Three shelves on each side, making six in total, with a gap in the middle forming a corridor reminiscent of a supermarket. She couldn't quite see the back of the room through the shelves. Turning to her left, she saw a rack behind a cage door filled with guns. She recognised a couple of shotguns and a few more of those same rifles Ben carried with him. A row of handguns and boxes of ammunition were stacked on more shelves.

Dee let out a whistle. "That's a lot of guns. I feel like I'm in the Matrix."

Ben grunted and walked with her towards Boss. "How's he doing?"

"Just concussed, I think. I gave him some painkillers, so he'll sleep it off."

"Good. I'm glad. Poor kid. He took a real knock to the head. If you want, I'll show you around my humble abode."

Dee nodded, only too glad for a distraction.

"It's no bomb shelter, but it's kept those Variants out so far. They're getting bolder each day."

Dee followed him to the back right-hand corner where two rooms were separated from the rest of the structure.

As Ben opened one door, he pointed to the other. "Bathroom with chemical toilet in there." He nodded towards the opened room. "In here is where the fun happens. This is the war room." He gestured for Dee to enter.

Dee gasped. A desk with four monitors and a keyboard lined the back wall. Two of the monitors were on and she could see camera feeds from outside. A stack of radio equipment lay on the table on the right-hand side, static hissing from the attached speakers. A large table covered in maps was set against the other wall. Dee could see Ben had been marking red Xs through the surrounding small towns, and the town of Cambridge was scribbled out.

"Wow, you're organised. But how are you getting power to run all this?"

"Solar. I've got a bank of them down the hill a bit. It's enough to keep this going, just. Also gives me a little hot water."

Dee went over to the map. "I suppose this means no survivors?" She pointed at the red Xs.

"Unfortunately, yes."

Dee traced the river north from Cambridge up to Hamilton. A big red X was drawn through it.

How had her basement group gone undetected? Not only from the Variants but from the collaborators too.

She looked at all the surrounding towns. Te Awamutu, Morrinsville, Huntly. All had red Xs through them. Dee rubbed her eyebrows and reached down to her neckline, desperate to feel the reassurance of the necklace Jack had given to her as an anniversary present.

So many red Xs. It started to really sink in just how

fortunate she and Boss had been.

Was it luck? Common sense? A bit of both? The Hemorrhage Virus had hit so fast, so furiously, that it had caught everyone but a few by surprise. She and Jack loved post-apocalyptic fiction. The more they read, the more they'd thought: *What if? What if something did happen?*

They'd thought they were prepared for it. But fate was a funny thing. They'd never taken into account where they would be when it hit.

Now Jack was God knows where and Dee was here. In a bunker. Safe. For now.

Ben took Dee back to the main living area, to all the shelving units stacked with supplies. Pointing to each row in turn, he said, "Food. Clothes. Survival gear, like tents, etc. Batteries, that sort of thing. I don't have any women's clothes, I'm afraid, but you're welcome to try and find something to fit. Feel free to have a shower too, but please, five minutes only. Very limited water supply."

"Ben, you're an angel." Dee's eyes filled with tears. "Thank you for your kindness, and for…" she gulped, unable to voice her thanks further, and waved her hands.

She could see Ben understood, his eyes growing soft. "You're welcome."

Dee nodded and started to select the smallest clothes she could find. Though little might fit her, she just wanted fresh clothes. She could still smell the stench of Missing Teeth on her. Shuddering in disgust, Dee headed to the shower.

— 22 —

The cool night air caressed Jack's skin, causing goosebumps. He leant his head back against the wall and looked down at the sleeping George. Smiling, Jack was amazed at how well the kid had adapted to this new hidey hole. They had hidden here since escaping and had eaten half the supplies from his pack. George had been resistant to the protein bar and beef jerky, but had devoured the chocolate.

Through the tiny window, Jack could see the moon. It was showing its half face. He estimated he had been down in this hell pit for eleven to twelve days. How had he survived with no water or food? For that matter, how had George? He was so small...so young at only eight (maybe) years old. So much for the rule of three, then.

Three weeks without food. Three days without water... Blah blah blah...

Jack could feel some life coming back into his body from the food and water and now felt confident enough to attempt an escape.

He needed a plan. As a teenager he'd been fascinated

by WWII escape stories. Had read the small town library out. The daring. The ingenuity. Both were incredible.

Gazing out the window, he could see his stars. His pinpricks of light. Millions of light years away.

There is always a way out of any situation.

All right, so we're in the hydro dam. Surrounded by monsters that want to eat us. A man is helping them. I've probably got two days' food at best. George's mum, Sarah, is missing. Dee is God knows where. It's dark and I don't even have any sunglasses on.

He couldn't help but grin at his movie reference. He couldn't even think of moving until at least midday, so he shifted his weight and closed his eyes. Nothing to be done till then.

Eat when you can. Sleep when you can. Be ready.

Jack woke to the sun shining in his eyes and George poking him in the arm.

"Mister. I really need to pee."

"Ummm, okay, buddy. Can you hold on a bit longer?" Jack said, rubbing the sleep from his eyes.

George started squirming, a panicked look on his face.

"I'm going to have to check if the coast is clear, all right?"

George nodded.

Jack jumped up on top of the lockers and searched the room. Seeing nothing, he reached down and lifted George up next to him. Pivoting, he dropped George down to the floor.

"Sorry, buddy. It will have to be in there," Jack said, pointing to the hand basin.

Jack checked his watch as George washed his hands. He decided to risk some exploration and guessed the room they were in was a couple of levels down. Jack didn't know the layout of the dam wall, but he trusted his instincts not to go down any deeper. He decided to stick to this level, for now.

George finished, and wandered back over to the lockers. Jumping down, Jack grabbed his hand. "We're going to go find your mum, okay. But we have to be super silent. We don't want to wake the monsters, do we?"

George pulled his hand away and twisted his fingers nervously, intertwining them in a wringing motion. "Nope," he murmured.

"Good. If they find us, you run, okay? You run in here and hide."

He continued to stare at George, waiting to see if he understood. His eyes were wide, pupils dilated. The sight broke his heart. The poor kid, having to live through this. He should be out playing. Running around. Gaming. Kid stuff.

Jack shook his head, angry at those responsible for ruining George's innocence. He embraced the anger. It gave him new energy.

He moved to the door into the room. Placing his ear against it, he listened for any sounds. He could smell that faint rotten fruit smell. It amazed him how it smothered even the stench of death. He cracked open the door and looked into the corridor. Seeing it was clear, he took George's hand and placed it around the waist belt of his pack.

"You hang on to this. Don't let go. Unless I tell you to run," Jack whispered.

"Okay," George said.

Not wanting to head back the way they'd originally

come, Jack headed in the opposite direction. Several other doors lined the corridor and a large green door stood at the end. More people were glued to the walls here, their faces oddly calm and serene as if in some sort of coma. He tried not to linger on their faces too long.

"Don't look at them, George. Look down," Jack said as he searched the people for blonde hair.

He felt George's grip tighten on the belt.

Tears pricked his eyes, a long-buried pain bubbling to the forefront of his mind. Jack had thought he had buried that particular memory deep, away, forgotten. He had avoided having his own children, limited his time with other people's kids. All to avoid the pain.

Jack loved his little brother, even though there was a ten-year gap. He was so full of life and curiosity. Jack read to him every night, played games, built forts.

As his brother grew, he introduced him to films, comics and the wonders of creativity and imagination.

Before the fateful trip to the snow.

Jack took his brother sledding. With each run, he squealed louder and louder.

"Higher, Jik Jik, higher!" he pleaded.

Caught up in his brother's delight, Jack relented. Took him to the very top of the steep hill.

Down they flew, getting faster and faster, the cold wind stinging their faces.

A fallen tree branch poking from the snow caught Jack's trailing foot, throwing him off.

The sled turned sharply. His brother slammed into the trees lining the hill.

Racing up, he found his loving little brother crumpled to one side, blood streaming down over his face, his little head crushed.

Jack cradled him and screamed until he was hoarse. That was how the paramedics found him.

They took his little brother away.

He never saw him again. The funeral directors advised Jack's mum to have a closed coffin.

Once an outgoing sixteen-year-old, Jack retreated within himself. Shutting away the world, he found solace and comfort in his books, his comics, his movies.

His mum sent him to see a psychiatrist. He went, begrudgingly. How could a stranger know his pain? Know his shame? Know his failing? His little brother was dead because of his error of judgement. His little brother was ashes in the wind because Jack'd been trying to impress his brother with his bravery.

But time heals all to a point, eventually. The psychiatrist helped Jack realise that it wasn't his fault. He hadn't put the branch there. To think more on the times he'd shared with his brother, the love, the laughter, the joy they'd brought to each other.

So Jack buried the guilt and the pain deep, deep down. Never forgetting the memory of his little brother, he learnt to live with it.

His brother's name had been George too. I'll save this one…

Wiping away the tears, Jack stopped at the first door and listened. Not hearing a sound, he tried the handle. Locked. Cursing silently, he quickly moved on to the next one. After several locked doors, he found an unlocked one. Opening it, Jack saw it was a maintenance room. A workbench lined one wall, with a peg board above filled with tools.

He couldn't hold back the exclamation that escaped his lips. Finally, a little luck. Grabbing some screwdrivers and a hammer, he jammed them into his belt.

If those things attack, at least I can go down fighting, give the kid a chance to run.

"What's this, Mister Jack?"

Jack looked down at George. He had crawled under the bench. He was holding out a rusty old machete, its wooden handle so cracked and pitted that someone had wrapped red electrical tape around it.

"That is a very dangerous weapon," Jack said, gently taking the machete out of the child's hands.

"But I want something to fight the monsters," George moaned.

Jack crouched down. "Okay, George, but let's find you something more suitable."

Jack searched the work area and found a tool belt. He placed it around George's waist, adjusting the strap as small as it could go. He populated it with chisels, screwdrivers and a small ball peen hammer.

"If they come, you stab and hit them as hard as you can, all right?" Jack demonstrated the motions.

George beamed up at him and nodded.

He knew the tools wouldn't do much good against those creatures; they were so damn fast, so ferocious. For that matter, he didn't know how long either of them would last. But a little hope and something to live for goes a long way.

"C'mon, kid. I don't know about you, but I want to get out of here."

"Mummy?"

"Yeah, we'll keep looking. Remember, super silent. If they come, run back to the red door and hide, okay?"

George pulled out his little hammer. "But I am Thor."

In spite of all the horror, the fear scratching at him,

Jack smiled at George. The kid's resilience was incredible. He just wanted to find his mum.

"Okay Thor. Let's go," Jack said, still smiling.

As they approached the green door at the end of the corridor, the stench of rotting fruit became overpowering. Jack's hand was shaking as he reached out and opened the door. Peering through the gap, he saw a sight that even the best horror writers' minds would struggle to imagine. Not wanting George to see, he spun the kid around, stood in front of him, and blocked the child's view.

Beyond the door, steel stairs descended into a cavernous area. Piles of bones, some with bits of tissue and sinews still attached, lay stacked in corners. Bits of people were strewn about, some half eaten. He could see torsos, arms, legs. Bones sticking out. One of the monsters was lying on top of a pile of intestines, covered in blood and plasma. Lining the walls of the room, severed heads in varying states of decay were on spikes made of bones.

In the deepest shadows of the room, Jack could see sleeping creatures. Some smaller creatures were nestled against some of the larger ones for warmth.

Jack paused, shocked. *Were they breeding? Already?*

He could see a particularly large stack of bones in the centre of the room. A throne of bones, reminiscent of one Jack had once seen in a catacomb in Europe.

The large mass moved. It was a massive creature, and plated bones protruded from its shoulders, forming spikes. A severed child's head had been placed atop each spike, much like some sort of grisly trophies. Fighting the bile rising up his throat, Jack turned away, his mind reeling. He had seen this creature before. When they were captured. It hadn't had the heads back then. The creature led, gave out orders.

Jack stumbled back, pushing George farther into the corridor. His eyes wandered lower. At the big creature's feet, blonde hair flowed over a woman's half-eaten body.

No! Sarah...!

Jack remembered, in a moment of clarity when he was drifting in and out of consciousness while trapped on the wall, that he had seen Sarah being taken. Taken for slaughter. All her past, present, and possible futures, snuffed out in an instant. In the end, she had become these monsters' sustenance.

George started screaming. Jack spun round. The boy was standing in the doorway, looking directly at his mother's remains.

As one, the creatures' heads swivelled around to face the door. Terrifying screeches echoed around the cavernous room. With stunning speed and agility, they leapt from the floor.

Jack pulled George away and slammed the door. Jamming one of his hammers through the handle, he hoped it would stop them for a moment, enough time to get away.

Grabbing the still-screaming George by his hand, he sprinted up the corridor, back towards the room they had sheltered in.

— 23 —

Behind Jack and George, wood and concrete splintered with a crash. Half-turning, Jack saw the monsters piling into the corridor, screeching and howling, saliva dripping from their sucker mouths. Muscles rippled beneath semi-translucent skin. They spotted Jack and George and howled as they bounded towards them.

George reached the red door first and was pulling it open when the next door down opened. The man with the red trucker's cap appeared, a stunned look on his face as he took in the unfolding chaos. Jack barrelled into him, taking him to the ground. The man bucked beneath him, shifting his weight in an attempt to throw Jack off. His hands flailed, desperate to get a hold on Jack.

Jack saw an opening and, without hesitation, rammed a screwdriver up under the man's chin, burying it deep into his brain. The man's eyes went wide with disbelief as Jack watched the life blink out.

Groping bastard!

A creature howled and leapt off the wall at Jack, claws extended. Jack twisted and threw himself through the door. But too slow. The creature raked its claws down his leg, tearing into his flesh. Screaming in pain, Jack stabbed down with the screwdriver, plunging it through the weird translucent skin and into its flesh. Gritting his teeth, Jack kicked out with his free leg, smashing the beast's head. The monster howled in anger, and clawed and scratched at Jack's torso. George, leaning over Jack, started whacking the monster on the head with his little hammer. The monster momentarily let Jack go to deal with this new annoyance, giving Jack the chance to kick out again. Freeing himself, Jack grabbed George, slammed the door closed and locked it.

Immediately, the creatures started throwing themselves at the door.

Throom, throom, throom. The sound of them hitting the door reverberated around the small room.

Ignoring the agony lancing up his body, Jack pulled himself to his feet. He knew the flimsy door and lock wouldn't hold the monsters out for long. Hobbling over to the metal lockers next to the door, he tried to tip them over.

"George, help me push!" he yelled.

George scrambled away from the noise of the beasts and stared at Jack.

"Push. Buddy. Please," Jack pleaded, straining with the weight of the locker.

George pushed against the metal side, and with their joint effort it crashed across the doorway.

"And this one too."

A second locker joined the first.

Exhausted from the fight and the effort of moving the lockers, Jack stood gasping. Blood continued to pour from his wounds and he was beginning to feel lightheaded. He knew he needed to stop the bleeding, at least temporarily. Sitting down with his back against the far wall, Jack taped up his wounds with the last of his duct tape. He could see they were deep.

God knows what bacteria and germs those things have on their claws. Will I become one of them?

The creatures continued to slam against the door. Jack could hear tearing sounds. They were beginning to tear the plasterboard walls surrounding the door.

Frantic, Jack looked around for an escape route. The small window was out; Jack had already tried it the day before. Welded shut, for some reason. The glass was reinforced with wire mesh.

They were trapped in a room with horrifying creatures attacking them, and with no way out. *The same as in Aliens...* Aliens! Suddenly, Jack had the answer. The ceiling! He looked at it. It was a false hanging ceiling made with cheap plaster tiles that could be individually moved.

Thanking his movie obsessions, and his knowledge of building materials, Jack grabbed George under his arms and hoisted him on top of the lockers. Jumping up, he pushed a tile up and to one side and poked his head through. Jack could see right across the rooms, and dividing the rooms were solid concrete walls with enough space to walk on.

Throom. Throom. Throom.

"C'mon, George." He grabbed the child and lifted him through into the ceiling cavity. "See that concrete bit? Run along to the end. Go! Now!"

Screeching, and then a huge rip, sounded from below as the monsters tore through the wall and into the room. Jack's heart leapt into his throat. With one final look below, he replaced the tile and turned to follow George, blood dripping off his boot and onto the ceiling tiles.

A monster smashed through the ceiling behind. If they hadn't been so dangerous, he'd have laughed as it got all tangled in the metal struts and wires. A red mist descended over Jack's vision. Pulling the rusty, red-handled machete from his belt, he lashed out at the nightmare's head, slicing into its neck and on, down through muscle and tissue. Black, gunky blood gushed over his hands. The machete stuck fast, lodged on the spinal column.

He pushed against the monster's chest, yanking the blade out.

Another one smashed its way through the ceiling.

Oh, you want some too!

He swung out with the machete, taking a big hunk of its face off.

"Jack! Jack!" George screamed.

More creatures started slamming through the ceiling.

"Run! I'm coming," Jack said. Taking a last swipe at the nearest creature, Jack half ran, half hobbled after George.

There! He could see sunlight streaming through a maintenance tunnel. He lifted George up and pushed him into it.

This red-haired kid, his chance at redemption.

Jack pushed himself through the tunnel, pain beginning to take its toll. Gritting his teeth, he fought through it. He wanted to find Dee so bad, to hold her again. Feel her soul. To sit on their couch and watch their favourite movies and talk into the night.

He and Dee could talk about anything. It was one of

the things he loved about her.

Jack glanced at George. Now he had someone else who needed him.

Dee would love him.

With the warmth of the sun on his battered body, Jack inhaled his first clean air in days, revelling in the scents; the river, the slight smell of decaying plants, even the lime from the surrounding concrete. He looked down at the boiling, bubbling river so far below. The spillways were open. They were standing in an opening halfway up the dam. On both sides, high cliffs led downriver. The rest of the concrete dam wall soared above them.

Screeching from above echoed around the sides of dam. The monsters howled, eager for their prey. The leader stared down at them, his huge muscles rippling under his bark-like skin. Severed heads on spikes, jiggled as he pointed at Jack and George, and howled.

Monsters ran down the dam from all sides, racing towards Jack and George. A dark avalanche of unstoppable sharp-toothed suckers and claws that made Jack's blood run cold.

Glancing quickly to his left, Jack grabbed George in a bear hug. "Take a deep breath buddy."

Filling his lungs, he leapt off the ledge and into the roaring water of the spillway.

Sorry kid. Better to drown than be torn apart.

I'm sorry, so sorry I've failed another George...

— 24 —

Dee couldn't believe how refreshed the shower made her feel. To wash all the stench, grime and dirt away after so many days. It was heavenly. She stood under the glorious hot water, for a time forgetting the repugnant Variants outside, the horrors of the last few days. Forgetting the sight of Faye being torn apart, of Rachel disappearing under a mass of Variants, her hand outstretched, her gasping, pleading for Dee to save her. She even forgot about Missing Teeth and his attempt to rape her.

The water washed away her fear and relaxed her tired mind.

Reluctantly she reached up, turned off the water and stepped out. Drying herself, she paused. Looking into the small mirror, she gazed at her gaunt reflection. Dee let out a bark of laughter at the sight of her collar bone poking out and she traced the curvature of her neck with her hand, surprised. She was happy to lose some extra pounds, but shocked at how quickly it had happened. With one last look at her lack of curves, she turned away from the mirror.

Dee pulled on her borrowed clothes, grateful to have

something clean against her skin. She headed back into the main section and checked on Boss. The swelling on his head seemed to be going down but the bruise was darkening. His breathing was shallow but steady.

Hearing Ben talking in the war room, Dee walked over.

"Yeah, that's correct, Falcon 1. I picked up two today. Over."

Hissing and static carried over the airwaves through the speakers. "Anything happening on the Variant front? Over."

"Heard some on my travels and the usual sniffing around my place. I had to take out two of them collaborators though. Over."

"All right, Dusty Hollow. Report in tomorrow. Over."

"SNAFU, Falcon 1. Wilco, Out."

Ben reached up. Switching off the radio, he turned to Dee. "Hey, howa you feeling?"

"Great. Thanks so much. You don't know how much I've been wanting a shower."

Dee was staring at the monitors and the camera feeds they showed. She could see several Variants moving across the feeds.

"You're not worried?" Dee said, pointing to the screens.

"Not really. I'm more worried about the ones I can't see. These ones are just looking for a way in, probing, looking for a weak spot. I don't get much sleep, though."

Dee could see from the bags under his eyes that Ben was telling the truth. Hell, no one got much sleep these days. Last night in the boat was the best sleep she'd had since all this began.

"Well, since I'm here, how about I watch for a few hours?"

"Yeah, maybe. We'll see how we go."

Dee looked back to the monitors and could now see at least twenty of the Variants roaming around, sniffing at everything. Searching.

"You're seriously not worried?"

Ben shook his head. "SNAFU."

"SNAFU? I heard you say that."

"It's military jargon. It means Situation Normal All Fucked Up. We use it sarcastically, meaning it's chaos, but that's normal."

"Oh right, so you were in the army?"

Ben nodded. "Yes, I served in the New Zealand Army, then the NZSAS, two tours of Vietnam, followed by some other stuff. Retired from the NZSAS when I was 45, then trained soldiers until I retired five years ago."

Dee looked into Ben's eyes. She could see pain buried deep. Those eyes had seen things no one should see. Not wanting to press him any further, Dee changed the subject. "Do you mind if I ask who you were talking too?"

"No, not at all. I was talking to the army...or what's left of it."

Ben pulled out a map of New Zealand. "We have pockets here in Wellington, holed up in the bunker under Government House. There's a small group in Auckland, under the museum. A few are scattered around the South Island, in the mountains. Most evacuated out to the islands with the navy. Here on the Chathams, Stewart Island, Great Barrier and Mayor Island."

"What about other survivors, like Boss and I?" Dee

asked, hopeful of news of Jack.

"A few, yes, when we can find them. We've been flying them out to Mayor Island."

"So why are you here?"

Ben rolled his shoulders, stretched out a kink and sighed. "Well, since I have this little bunker, I was recalled to active duty and ordered to stay behind, hunt for survivors."

Dee allowed hope to float back into her mind. Perhaps Jack was still alive. Maybe he had been airlifted to safety.

"Can we radio Mayor Island and ask about my husband, Jack?"

"It's pretty chaotic over there, but sure, let's go for it."

He turned back to the bank of radios and turned one on. He turned the detent dial until he had the right frequency, then pushed down the talk button on the microphone.

"Falcon 7, Falcon 7, this is Dusty Hollow, over."

A voice immediately answered, making Dee's heart leap with excitement.

"Falcon 7 receiving. Over."

"Falcon 7, looking for civvie, maybe brought a few days back. Over."

"Name, Dusty Hollow? Over."

Ben looked at Dee. "Jack, Jack Gee. G-E-E."

"Falcon 7, civvie's name is Jack Gee, that's Golf-Echo-Echo. Over."

"Received. We'll get back to you. Out."

Dee paced around the room, grinning from ear to ear. She had hidden in that damp, stinky basement for thirteen days, and in the house for two. Fear of getting torn apart and eaten had frayed her nerves. But she had survived. Boss had provided humour. Her hope of seeing Jack had never diminished but now it flared up anew, thanks to Ben. He looked like a gentle giant, but Dee had seen the ruthless former SAS soldier in action.

Ben looked at Dee, a twinkle in his brown eyes. "Wait a minute. Is your married name 'Gee'?"

Dee laughed. "Yes, I know. Dee Gee."

"Really?" Ben smirked. He leant back and chortled.

"Yeah." Dee giggled. It felt good to share a laugh with Ben.

The radio crackled to life. Dee's heart hammered in her chest. "Dusty Hollow, Dusty Hollow, this is Falcon 7, Over."

"Receiving Falcon 7. Over."

"Nobody of that name on the civilian manifests, Dusty Hollow. Out."

She was devastated. She had allowed herself to hope. Hope Jack had made it to Mayor Island. She sat down in a chair, deflated. The roaring in her ears drowned out the rest of the radio conversation.

Ben put a reassuring hand on her shoulder. "I'm sorry Dee, I really am. I'll get you and Boss to the next airlift."

Dee nodded numbly, eyes downcast. "I should have gone to him. He was in the bush. But I made him come to me."

"Dee, where was he?"

"Up in the Kaimai Mountains. Near Sentinel Rock."

Ben got up and started pacing around the small room. "So he would've come across the country towards the city, right?"

Dee could feel a spark of excitement. "Yeah. He loves those back country roads."

Ben fumbled through his pile of maps. Finding the one of the surrounding area, he excitedly pointed down. "Look. All the roads got choked up quickly, so maybe he had to skirt this area, forcing him wide to try to come into the city from the south?"

Dee nodded her head in agreement.

"If he ran into any Variants, he may have been taken."

Ben placed both gnarled hands on Dee's shoulders. "Dee, I think I might know where he is. If he's alive, he's here."

Dee looked at the map. Ben was pointing at the Waikato River. Next to his finger, she read *Karapiro Dam*.

"The dam? Why would he be there?"

"Those guys you met? Well, they used to find survivors too, only they give them to the Variants. I captured one of the traitors and extracted some information. The Variants use the dam as a meat locker, a slaughterhouse and a bloody nest!" Ben spat the last words. "Look. I'm not going to lie to you. It's a long shot. Chances are he just got caught up in the chaos."

Dee felt herself fall to the ground. Food? Her Jack, now food? The mere thought of it curdled her stomach. She could feel tears welling up in her eyes and she buried her head in her hands. Dee didn't want Ben to see her like this. Soldiers like him were used to people holding their emotions in check.

Ben grasped her shoulder. "If we had a way to be sure, I'll help you get him."

"Wait. You said it's a meat locker?"

"Yes."

"So, that means there are other people there?" Dee said, rising to stand next to Ben. A plan was forming in

171

her mind.

"That's the impression I got from the traitor, yes," Ben said, grimacing.

"Why doesn't the army mount a rescue mission, then?"

"I've already asked and got a firm no. Not enough resources."

"That's crazy," Dee said. "I thought the army was there to protect the citizens. To protect our way of life. Not run and hide."

Ben smiled and nodded. "I agree with you, Dee. I must admit I don't like this running and hiding."

Dee paced the room, arms clasped behind her back. There were so many thoughts running through her head, she struggled to focus. She tried to calm herself and then, with sudden clarity, an idea came to her. But with no knowledge of how the electrical grid worked, it was a long shot.

She stopped walking and snapped her head up, looking at Ben. "You don't happen to have an Android phone charger, do you?"

— 25 —

Dee watched as Ben rummaged around in the drawers on the desk.

"Is this what you mean?" Ben said, holding up the charger.

Dee looked at the end and smiled. "Yes."

She plugged it in and ran back to the bathroom, where she had left her old, smelly clothes. When she had been resting in the boat, Dee had been surprised to find her smartphone in her pocket. She guessed she had put it there out of habit. Or, and more likely, hoping for a miracle, that Jack would call her.

Thankfully her phone sprang to life and Dee spent a few seconds scanning through her apps.

"What are you going to do? Call him?" Ben said, frowning.

Dee shook her head. "No. Tried that already. I'm going to use this app. *Find my phone.* Jack installed it in case he ever went missing on one of his hikes."

"Good idea."

"I just hope the cell towers have power."

"I'm pretty sure they have backup."

Dee grunted and stared at her screen. The app glowed

back at her, but after several moments a tiny blue arrow blinked back. Dee swiped her fingers over the map, enlarging it. Jack's phone was on Wiltsdown Road. Dee heart sank as she glanced over the map. That was at least thirty kilometres away from Karapiro. She showed Ben the location.

"Damn it," Ben said. He stroked his beard and looked over his paper maps. "Dee. He could still have ended up in the dam. Look how close his phone is to the river. Maybe he ran into trouble and had to leave it in a hurry."

"Do you think there's a chance?"

"Stranger things have happened," Ben replied. He tapped his fingers on the desk. "There's always a chance."

"I have to know, Ben. I can't fly out of here to Mayor Island without knowing," Dee said. "Will you help me search for him."

Ben looked at her, a steely glint in his eyes. "I never could say no to a pretty lady asking for help."

"So that's a yes?"

"Affirmative. We'll need guns. Lots of them." Ben laughed. "What about the kid?"

"I'll ask him when he wakes up."

Dee and Ben spent the rest of the evening making preparations. Planning a possible rescue was not something Dee had ever thought she would be doing, but the thought of her Jack being stored as food to be consumed was not something she could bear to imagine. This guy, who through kindness and a quirky sense of humour had helped her through the darkness. This guy who, through sharing his joy of movies, books and the natural world had helped Dee see the magic of the universe. She wasn't going to give up on him. She had to know, and if she could banish some of these monsters to the pit of hell from whence they came, all the better.

As she helped Ben prepare, she checked on Boss a few times but the poor kid just slept right through. Even with all the noise they were making.

Ben spent thirty minutes showing Dee how to use an AR-15. How to load it, where the selector was. How to keep her finger on the guard, not the trigger. Dee tried to remain attentive, but exhaustion crept in. The bunks in the next room looked more and more inviting.

"Ben?"

"Yeah?"

"Can we continue this in the morning?"

"All right, sure. And Dee, don't worry. We'll go find him."

She could see the genuine belief in Ben's eyes. It comforted her, but that old demon of self-doubt nagged at the back of her mind, threatening to pull her back down.

"Wake me for my watch, okay?"

"Sure."

Dee lay awake for some hours, her body battered and bruised but her mind racing, thinking out all the scenarios. *What if Jack is dead? Could I still go on? What chance do we have?* Sleep finally pulled her into its embrace.

Dee woke to Boss shaking her shoulder. "Hey, sleeping beauty. Where are we?"

Pushing herself up, Dee struggled to shake the cobwebs from her mind. "Umm, we're safe...Ben...saved us...his place."

"Ben?"

Dee ran her hands through her pixie hair, pulling out the knots. "It's okay." She patted Boss on the shoulder. "He's a friend."

"What happened?" Boss said. He rubbed the bruise on his head.

"After you were knocked out, Ben shot those two rapists and brought us here. Come on, I'll introduce you."

"Did those guys… Umm?"

"No. Ben shot them before they could." Dee smiled.

"I'm sorry, Dee. I tried to help but he was too strong," Boss said, wiping away a tear.

"Boss. You tried and you put yourself on the line to save me. Thank you." She pulled Boss into a hug and held on to him.

After a couple of seconds, Dee let go. "Come, I'll introduce you to Ben."

Boss grinned and followed her into the war room. Ben turned as he heard them walk up. Dee could see his eyes were red and slightly puffy.

"Hey. You should have woken me for my watch."

"It's all right. You guys looked exhausted, thought I'd give you some rest."

"Still, you need it too."

Ben tilted his head to one side. "I'm used to it. Been surviving on little sleep most of my working life. This must be Boss?"

Dee smirked. "Oh yes, sorry. Ben, Boss, Boss, Ben."

"Thank you for yesterday," Boss said, holding out his hand.

"That's all right kid." Ben shook the offered hand. "Hungry?"

"You have food?"

Ben grinned and slapped Boss on the back.

Dee watched the exchange, admiring how they accepted each other so quickly. She guessed the apocalypse could bring out the worst and the best in people.

Before the Hemorrhage Virus had torn into the fabric of society, throwing the country into chaos, she never would've imagined herself doing any of the things she had done in the last couple of weeks.

Deep down inside is a strength most of us never know exists until the greatest of circumstances call upon it. That time is now. Today it is time.

After a hearty breakfast of bacon, eggs and sausages, Boss started to look more like his old self. Dee grinned as she finished her meal and her cup of coffee, sighing inwardly at the bitter taste. It had been days since she had enjoyed a cup.

"What's the plan, Ben?" Dee said, glancing at the soldier.

"Plan?" Boss said. "What have you guys been up to?"

"We might know where Jack is."

Boss frowned and looked between her and Ben. His mouth opened and closed like a goldfish. "I'm trying to think of some witty Python reference but I've got nothing. Just. What?"

"C'mon, I'll show you," Dee said, pushing back her chair.

Ben gathered them around the table in his war room and spread out one of the maps. Ben filled Boss in on what they had figured out while he'd been unconscious, then outlined his plan.

"This is the nest where we think Jack is. There are

multiple entrances but only three of us.

"Boss, you're going to be in the river driving the boat you two found. Dee and I are going to go in, look for Jack and get out, killing as many of those bastards we can. As you discovered, these things don't like the water for some reason, so that's our escape route. Now, I'm not going to sugarcoat it: this is probably a suicide mission, and I'm disobeying orders. But I'm tired of the army just running and hiding." Ben looked sternly at Dee then Boss. "I'm giving both of you the opportunity to back out now. I know neither of you have training, but someone with determination and a will to survive can overcome great odds."

Dee put her hand over Boss's. "I know it's a lot to ask, Boss. If you don't want to do this, it's fine."

Boss nodded, shrugged. "Sure, why not, I'm in. Two weeks ago I was just another millennial playing video games and annoying my parents. It's better to burn out than to fade away, eh?"

She couldn't help but grin at his movie reference. Just like Jack. Probably why she liked the kid so much.

"Thanks, Boss. I appreciate it," Dee said, smiling. She looked back down at the map and remembered Jack's phone.

"Shouldn't we check the phone location first, in case he's moved. Ben?"

Ben crouched down and opened a big duffle bag next to the table. Pulling out some guns, he placed them on the table. "My gut says he's in the nest. We can check it after."

"Okay. Thank you."

"All right. Boss, you're going to take these in the boat

as backup. If we get out of there alive and Variants are attacking us, as I know they will be, you're going to have to give us covering fire. Don't worry too much about hitting them. Just give them something to worry about. I'll give you both some quick lessons before we move out at 1100 hours, okay?"

Dee and Boss nodded. Ben pulled out a rifle, the same as the one Dee had seen him use in their rescue.

"This is for you, Dee. Again, I'll give you another quick lesson before we go, okay? I'll also give you a shotgun — easier to hit them with. Now, if we get out alive, Boss, you fish us out of the river and we motor to the vehicle I'm going to drop off here." He pointed to a spot on the map. "Then we hightail up this road straight to this airfield. I'll call in the chopper to get us out to Mayor Island."

Dee looked at Ben and saw a determined look. She felt happier knowing he was a seasoned professional. It was an extremely simple plan, but as he was the only one with military training, it was the only course of action to take. If Jack was out there, she had to know.

"Umm, why can't we wait for your army buddies?" Boss said.

"They would never approve it. The order went out about a week ago. Get out with as many survivors as you can find or hunker down. The virus hit too fast. The under-strength army wasn't ready for this. It was a miracle the navy and air force were having exercises in the Pacific. As harsh as it sounds, they aren't worried about one man. It's us or no one will save Jack," Ben said.

"Fine. Let's go hunt some Orcs!" Boss smirked.

Dee shook her head at the teenager. Definitely like

Jack. Movie obsessed.

At 1100 hours Dee found herself following Ben back down the same road they had driven up the previous day. She couldn't help but shudder in disgust as they pulled into the farm where Missing Teeth and his buddy had tried to rape her.

Dee and Boss climbed out of the vehicle and headed towards the boat. Dee hugged the teenager goodbye before he climbed in.

As he moved out into the current, she waved. "Good luck... Thanks, Boss."

Boss returned the wave. "Now you owe me."

Jumping back into the car, Dee found herself grinning as she followed Ben again.

The sun was reaching its peak and she revelled in the warmth of its rays. She couldn't help but wonder if this was the last time she would feel them on her skin. That she was on her farewell drive, taking in her last sight of the world they had lost. Dee wound down her window and let the wind blow through her hair, enjoying the sensation. Jack always said to enjoy the little things.

They broke the world and ripped my life apart. I'm going to do my best to take back what's mine.

Don't give up hope, Jack. It's all we've got left.

— 26 —

Jack fought against the strong undertow and currents. He kicked to the surface, pulling George with him. He cradled the child in a lifesaver's embrace and gulped for air. With the added weight of George, Jack realised that his backpack had to go. Grunting with the effort he managed to slip off one strap, then the other. Finally the pack slid from his shoulders. He watched as it bobbed in the swirling river and the current swept it away towards the bank. He would miss it. It had been a good friend for some years now, since Dee had given it to him as a gift.

The cacophony of screeches and howls broke into his thoughts as the torrent drove him away from the dam, lessening the roar of flowing water. He closed his eyes briefly, cursing silently. For a second there, everything had been normal. When he opened them again, he couldn't miss the monsters. They were racing along the tops of the steep cliffs on either side of the river, keeping up with his and George's progress downstream. The thick undergrowth barely slowed them as they took to the trees, swinging from branch to branch and leaping over rocks as if they weren't there.

Jack kicked hard, willing the current to move him

down the river faster. The sun was getting high in the sky now. He hoped it would force the monsters back to their nest. As he floated, the creatures continued their relentless pursuit, screeching at him. Every now and then he heard the almighty bellow of the leader. He could just picture it, weird bark skin and spiked shoulders, and the grotesque child-head trophies. Jack couldn't see him, but he would never forget the sight of the two decaying children's heads displayed, jiggling with the beast's every movement.

Frantically he searched for a way out. They had made it this far. Alive, bruised, broken and injured — well, he was — but alive. He didn't want to give up now. He had fought to break away from his cocoon. He had found some salvation in George. He had discovered the reason behind their capture. They had escaped. All this would be for nothing if he didn't find a way for them to reach safety.

Feeling George nestled into his chest, hanging on to him for any sort of comfort, confirmed it. He was thankful. Thankful for this chance at redemption. Jack looked around. He had trained as a lifesaver in his youth, but with all the trauma his body had gone through, he wouldn't last much longer in the river.

Farther down, he could still see the limestone cliffs soaring high. At the bottom, little pockets of bank had eroded away to form muddy coves covered in a thick tangled mess of tree roots and scrub. He could see the bright green of his hiking pack floating close by.

As far as Jack could see, there weren't any monsters in the scrub. Their screeches sounded close, though. He really needed to get out of the river. Risking it, he kicked towards one of the muddy coves and his pack. Pushing George in front of him, he pulled his exhausted body out of the river, hooking his leg through the strap of his pack as he did so. To have any chance at survival, he needed his pack, so he was thankful it had been waiting. Cold water dripped off his head, splattering onto the mud. Jack was having trouble focussing on his immediate surroundings. He realised the last few days were taking their toll. Wiping river water from his eyes, he crawled under the mess of roots. Exhausted, he leaned up against the tree and took a few deep breaths.

George sat panting, his eyes flicking around.

"It's okay, George," Jack said. "We're going to hide for a while."

Jack looked down at the thick mud coating his legs and arms and smiled. He could just hear Dee laugh at him and say. *"You and your movies."*

He scooped up handfuls of mud and started to coat George with it. "Sorry, buddy. I know it's cold and gross, but we need to hide from the monsters."

Jack made sure the kid was completely covered before doing himself. *Maybe it will work.* It was worth a shot.

The creatures clearly had excellent vision and a heightened sense of smell, not to mention exceptional hearing. As exhausted as he was, he knew that if he wanted any chance of getting down the river, they had to hide out for now and rest.

They had achieved the impossible: they had escaped hell.

Since learning of the virus, Jack had been trying to get home to Dee. They had always had a "what if?" plan. But no amount of planning and preparation had readied him for the horrors that hunted him now. He had always been a keen outdoors type and had learned the hard way that you needed to be prepared for anything.

One spring day, a day hike turned into a three-day nightmare. The weather was cool, clear and crisp as he set off on his six-hour return hike up one of the many valleys cutting their way through the mountains close to his home.

The trip up the valley passed without incident. On the return journey, he slipped on a wet rock and caught his boot on a tree root. The result was that he broke his ankle as he tumbled down a steep ravine.

Jack shouted for help until he lost his voice. He had broken the cardinal rule: he hadn't told anyone of his intentions.

With little hope of rescue, Jack spent the next three days crawling out of the ravine, and then farther down the river to the more popular walking tracks. A very surprised group of elderly hikers found an extremely dehydrated and hungry Jack.

The relief had been immense. He had learned his lesson. Now he followed a strict code of conduct.

Always be prepared.

Branches behind Jack snapped as the creatures shrieked and howled around him. Answering howls joined the monsters as they ran up and down the river hunting for their lost prey. Jack glanced down at George who had his knees tucked under him and eyes clenched shut. Jack prayed for his mud trick to work. It was all he had left. He had no weapons apart from the machete. If the creatures did find them, he figured he could maybe kill one; at a stretch, two.

The closest monster let out a screech, its pitch

deafening. Jack held George's hand tight as the mud-covered kid snuggled into him, shaking. Closer now, the screeching intensified. Jack struggled to keep himself from shaking.

Go away...go away...go away...

A howl right above him nearly made him jump back into the flowing water. Opening his eyes, he checked his escape route. Looking out at the river, Jack couldn't believe his eyes.

A large motorboat was slowly making its way up towards the dam. He wanted to yell out a warning to the tall, brown-haired figure. It was hard to tell, but Jack thought he looked to be only a teenager.

The figure glanced from side to side, watching the howling monsters on top of the cliffs. Jack could see he was being careful to keep the boat in the middle of the river.

With a horrific screech, the creature above Jack tore off after the boat, following it back towards the nest.

Holding a trembling George, Jack rocked the boy back and forth, trying to soothe him.

"It's okay, they've gone for now," he whispered. "We're going to eat the last of my food, then we're going to have to get back in the river, all right?"

George whimpered into Jack's chest.

Watching the disappearing boat, Jack wondered what the hell the kid on the boat was thinking?

Has the whole world gone mad?

— 27 —

Dee stared at the hydro dam as Ben pulled to the side of the road and brought the 4x4 to a stop. She could see the dam stretching across the river, a high cliff dropping away on the opposite bank.

A small electrical substation nestled against the side of the bank she stood on, and beyond, a road stretched across the dam wall, following its curve.

"We go in there, nice and slow," Ben said. He was pointing at the larger building below the substation. "Shoot anything that's not human. Go for their centre mass to bring them down, then once in the head, okay?"

Dee nodded. "Got it. Rule two. Double tap."

"If they attack en mass, just fire until you've got nothing left. When you reload, shout it so I can cover you."

Dee looked at Ben. She was determined but scared. Scared of failing. Failing to find Jack. Scared of dying. Dying without knowing what had happened to him. To anyone she cared about. She sighed and looked down at the AR-15, feeling the weight of it.

Ben placed a hand on her shoulder. "Just point and

shoot, kid. Give them hell. We find Jack, we retreat straight away."

Dee followed close behind Ben as they crept up to the large set of wooden doors. She could detect the rotten fruit smell that lingered around the beasts, a sure indicator they were here. Taking a deep breath, she readied herself.

Ben reached out and tried the handle. It gave. Dee watched as he pushed the door wider. She took a last deep breath to help centre herself and followed him through. She took up a covering position like they had practised back at the bunker. Scanning the small room, she could see a little desk to one side but no other furniture.

Ben indicated with his head for her to cover him. He opened up the next door, revealing a steel set of stairs going down. The reek of rotten fruit made Dee gag. Another stench wafted in. She wasn't quite sure, but it reminded her of decaying flesh.

The thought of what lay beyond, at the bottom of the stairs, horrified her. Ben looked at her, his eyes asking if she was all right. She nodded, and they descended into the stench.

Opening the door at the bottom of the stairs, Dee saw what true horror looked like in the corridor beyond. People were stuck to the walls, trapped in some weird membrane. Cocooned. Their faces serene. Her heart pounded, her breath quickened. Praying for her Jack, she frantically ran down the corridor, searching the faces for him. She ignored Ben's pleading for her to slow down.

On she ran, searching. With each successive stranger's face, her hope of finding Jack alive dwindled. She nearly tripped over the body of a man, blood pooled around his head. Letting out a gasp, she dropped to her knees and pulled the body over. Not recognising the face, Dee let the pent-up tears flow.

Ben reached down and hauled her to her feet. "We have to keep going." He gestured down the long corridor.

Dee wiped away her tears. "I thought it was him for a moment." She gripped her rifle tighter, feeling the anger building in her body. Seeing the fate of these people drew up the hate that had dwelled deep down for so long. Dee had learned long ago to control that instinct. But seeing this place brought it out. She wanted to make those responsible pay. To exterminate them.

Dee and Ben made their way farther down the corridor, Ben covering as Dee searched the faces. The stench of death and decay became overpowering as they reached a large green door. It stood ajar, splintered on both sides of the door jamb.

Ben poked his head around the door. She saw his eyes go wide in horror.

Screeching erupted from the room, chilling her. Ben spun to Dee. "Run now, fast! Go!"

Dee turned to run. The screeching grew louder. Ben slammed the useless door and brought his rifle up to his shoulder.

The Variants smashed through the broken door and Ben opened fire. Firing quick bursts, he quickly took down the first three. Dee raised her own weapon as she turned to help and aimed for a Variant crawling up the wall beside them. She fired, hitting it right in its torso and taking a chunk off one of its weird claw-like appendages. She watched, amazed, as it kept coming at her. Firing again, she blasted it straight in the throat. The Variant slumped to the ground, dead. More Variants replaced it.

Man, these things are fast.

The next few minutes became a blur of terror. Dee fired again and again into the writhing mass of hell, but still they came.

She went into a state of automatic trance. Aim, fire, reload, repeat.

While she was reloading, a Variant crawled over the body of one she had dropped and raked its claws down her leg.

Screaming out in agony, Dee smashed the stock of the AR-15 into its head. Again and again she bashed it. Black blood oozed out of its head but still it came. It screeched and slashed at her with its claws. The creature smacked its sucker mouth together and flicked out a forked tongue.

Dee slung the rifle over her shoulder and drew her katana. She lunged and speared the Variant through the throat. The black, gunky blood gushed out over her hands. She watched the demon light leave its eyes and she grunted with relief.

Dee looked around for Ben. He was firing into the last group and finally dropped the last two Variants with a quick burst. Ben looked over to Dee clutching her leg.

"You all right?"

"I'll live, I think."

"Good. C'mon. Time to leave."

Dee shook her head. "I need to find Jack."

"I'm sorry Dee, I really am, but I think he's gone."

"You don't know that!" Dee shouted.

Ben moved closer and placed a hand on her shoulder. "No, I don't, but you need to live. If not for you, then do it for Jack. Carry on, for him."

Dee shook her head again, harder this time. "I'm not leaving without knowing," she said and brushed past Ben.

Dee had taken a few steps down the corridor when a terrifying screech caused both of them to turn. Several Variants were approaching from the direction in which she and Ben had entered. More screeches and howls answered them. Looking over Ben's shoulder, she could see a door with a red sign. The walls had been smashed in on both sides of the door.

Ben turned and saw what Dee was looking at. "Go! Yes!"

Bursting into the room through one of the holes in the wall, Dee saw a barricade made from metal lockers. *Jack?* Hope to find her husband alive in this den of terror returned. She clambered up on top of the lockers. Ben started firing at the screeching Variants.

"Ben, up here!"

She racked her shotgun and blasted at the Variants as they clambered through the holes. Ben was struggling to haul himself up as he turned and fired another burst.

She blasted another Variant, the sound deafening as it echoed off the walls of the small room.

A Variant screeched and, launching itself through the air, latched on to Ben's back, digging its claws in deep.

Dee let out a howl in frustration and anger, jammed her shotgun into its sucker and blew its head off, showering both of them in brains and black gunk.

"Thank you," Ben said, pulling himself up.

They climbed into the ceiling, turning and firing as they went. Variants continued to pour through the holes, chasing after them.

Dee reached a small tunnel with light shining through.

Blood had pooled on the floor next to the entrance.

Jack? Are you alive?

"Get in the tunnel, NOW!" Ben yelled at her, pulling her back into reality.

Dee didn't argue. She threw herself into the tunnel and crawled through to the end.

Ben jumped in after her. The Variants pursuing them tore at the concrete surrounding the tunnel as they tried to follow the fleeing humans. They ripped at each other in their desperation. They could have fitted easily but, in their crazed hunger lust, their cognitive thoughts were abandoned. The Variants fought each other. Dee smiled and crawled farther down the passage.

One of the Variants crammed itself in. Shrieking, it tried to tear Ben apart.

Ben fired into its head point blank, silencing it.

"Dee, get ready to jump, okay? Into the river!"

Shell-shocked from the last twenty minutes, she nodded.

Ben reached into his vest and took out a small grenade. He joined Dee at the entrance and grabbed her in a hug.

"Fire in the hole," Ben shouted. He threw the grenade and launched into the river.

Dee felt the shockwave of the grenade as she fell towards the water, wrapped in the embrace of this gentle giant. Before she hit the water, she saw Boss coming upriver in the boat and grinned. She was still alive.

— 28 —

Jack took out the last of his meagre supplies and shared them with George. The poor kid sat hugging his knees, rocking back and forth. Jack wasn't surprised. It had been a hell-filled few days for them both; he felt like doing the same. Watching George, Jack wanted more than anything to survive, to find Dee. To keep George safe.

After going through so much, and fighting every step of the way, he didn't want to give in now, no matter how hopeless it seemed.

There is always a way out.

Jack sat listening for the creatures' howls but could only hear them in the distance. Crawling out of their muddy root cave, he pulled George up and lifted him onto the bank.

Pop... Pop... Pop.

Jack spun around, back towards the dam. That was gunfire. Muffled, but definitely gunfire.

Hesitating, he listened as it intensified. The sounds of two distinct gunshots came down the river, reverberating off the limestone cliffs. *Perhaps some kind of rifle?* Jack couldn't be sure. Then the unmistakable boom of a shotgun rang out. He recognised that straight away. His mind jolted back to a memory of Dee teaching him how to hold the gun against his shoulder. She patiently taught him how to line up the target. How to squeeze the trigger in between breaths.

Those idiots are going to bring that whole nest out…

Jack stood rooted to the spot, listening to the battle. He glanced around at the creatures as they ran howling and screeching back to the dam. Finally Jack looked down the river. "Hang on to this George, okay?" Jack said as he looped the much lighter pack over the boy's shoulders.

The two of them waded back out into the river. He nestled George in the lifesaver's embrace once again and let the current take them downstream, away from the gunfight. Away from the madness. Jack saw it as a slim window of opportunity. Flee while the creatures were distracted.

He could see the sun poking through the fluffy white clouds, its rays reflecting off the river and into his eyes. Jack wondered why the monsters were out in the midday sun. Normally they hid from its strong UV light.

A loud *BOOM* echoed down the river, breaking him from his thoughts.

Was that explosives? Hell. Whoever was at the dam, they were serious.

Jack heard the motorboat engine revving and turned his head, searching out the craft. It tore around the corner, the throaty sound of its engine reverberating around the cliffs.

The monsters' howls and screeches followed. Jack's eyes were drawn up. Fascinated, he watched as a black mass flowed out of every entrance of the dam and buildings. The creatures poured out of the doors. Windows. Tunnels. Everywhere. There had to be hundreds of them now. Standing near the back of the mass was the Alpha leader. It towered above the monsters. Arms outstretched like some evil priest, it urged its brethren on.

Jack raised his free arm, trying to signal the speeding boat. It was only a few metres away. He ducked under the water as it swerved around him. Jack spat out river water and hugged George closer. The craft slowed and fishtailed around. Jack could see the tall teenager and a bearded man looking at him. Slumped in the back of the boat was a smaller figure.

"Help, please... I have a boy," Jack said, raising his tired voice.

The boat floated towards him. Or was he floating towards it? Coaxing his exhausted arms, he held George up. The bearded man frowned and hauled George into the boat.

Strong, gnarled hands grasped Jack's and pulled him out of the water. "What the hell are you doing in the water?"

Jack flicked his eyes back to the dam and nodded. "Thank you," he gasped.

The howls and screeches of the creatures became deafening, so loud they shuddered through Jack. He glanced up as the creatures started throwing themselves into the river like suicidal lemmings. The monsters had lost their fear of the water. His heart sank. Just for a fraction of a second he had thought he was safe.

"Boss. Get us out of here!" the bearded man yelled as he raised his rifle and began firing.

Jack felt the bow of the boat lift as the teenager opened the throttle, and he grabbed whatever he could hold on to.

He watched in horror as more and more monsters threw themselves from the cliffs, trying to reach the fleeing boat. A few managed to land on the boat. Digging their claws in, they scrambled and tore into the skin of the boat, their yellow eyes glaring at the humans.

The bearded man swung his rifle and fired. Calmly taking them out.

"Dee. We need you. Snap out of it!"

Despite everything happening around him…the boat speeding down the river…the gun rapidly firing…the creatures' howling and trying to eat him…time slowed down for Jack. *Dee? Here? After all that? Is this real?*

Turning to the stern of the boat, Jack looked into those beautiful eyes staring back at him.

Covered in mud, blood and God knows what else, he launched himself into the arms of the one person who meant the most to him in the world. His rock, his shelter from the storm.

All those years alone had been worth it to spend the last three with her. She was a woman of beauty, intelligence and magic. She had taught Jack so much about life, about ways to appreciate it.

Even after these nightmares had torn his world apart, he had never given up hope of finding her again. It had been his motivation, his energy. His one ring. He had kept the image of her in the forefront of his mind. Those long, confused hours stuck to the wall. Through everything. Dee's beautiful eyes and smiling face had kept him going.

Jack embraced Dee and sobbed. Holding her against his body, he was afraid to let go.

"I thought I had lost you," Jack said, kissing her cheek.

"Me too," Dee said.

"Dee. Come on!" shouted the bearded man.

Dee pulled herself out of Jack's embrace and, racking her shotgun, started blasting at anything that moved in the water.

"Jack. In that bag. Grab a gun!" Dee said, gesturing with her head.

Jack found the bag and unzipped it. There were half a dozen guns that he didn't recognise and two shotguns. He hadn't fired a shotgun for a few months, not since that day at the firing range shooting clay pigeons. Jack gritted his teeth.

He looked around him. At the howling monsters throwing themselves into the river. At the little red-haired boy, George, huddled against a seat. At his wife, Dee, firing into the black mass of monsters. At the teenager steering the boat down the river. At the bearded man, rifle held to his shoulder, firing quick, controlled bursts.

Each of these people was fighting, fighting to stay alive. Fighting for the human race.

Jack checked the safety was off, and shells were loaded. Planting his feet, he tried to get his balance in the moving boat. Frustration boiling up, he joined the fight.

The Variants continued to throw themselves into the river. A couple more managed to land on the bow of the boat, but between himself, the bearded man and Dee, they dealt with them quickly.

The boat swung from side to side, dodging the beasts. Jack fired at a creature swimming towards him, taking off part of its head. He grimaced as it sank under the waves. Jack glanced up, searching for another target. The river in front of him was clear.

"Go!" Jack said, pointing.

The teenager heard him and opened the throttle, launching the boat free of the raining terrors.

As the boat pulled away, a loud bellow echoed down the cliffs. Jack shook his head and looked up at the Alpha. It glared down at the fleeing humans. With one last bellow he turned away, and his army of demons followed, howling and screeching.

Jack saw the bearded man raise his rifle and look through the scope, but he held his shot.

For now, they were clear of the creatures. The boat sped down the wide muddy river. Soon the high limestone cliffs gave way to rolling farmland.

"Why didn't you shoot?" Dee said as she hugged Jack.

"No point. I don't think this calibre would penetrate all that bone and hide," Ben said. He lowered the weapon and glanced at them. "I guess this is Jack?"

A smile broke out on Dee's face. "Yeah, it sure is." She squeezed Jack tighter.

Jack caught her gaze. He knew what she was thinking. Somehow amongst the insanity, they had found each other. He could once again look into those blue eyes.

"Ben, Jack, Jack, Ben. And the tall one driving is Boss," Dee said.

Jack and Ben acknowledged each other with a nod before shaking hands.

"Thank you. How did you know where I was?" Jack asked, shaking his head.

"A bit of guesswork. A bit of technology and a lot of luck," Ben said. "I asked one of the collaborators what they were up to. He told me about the nest. When Dee came along looking for you, I figured it was the first place to look."

"Thanks," Jack said. He glanced down at Dee and raised an eyebrow. "Technology?"

"Find My Phone," Dee said. "Your phone is thirty kilometres upriver."

"Yeah. I crashed the car and ran into some of those beasts."

Jack cast his eyes down. With all that had happened, it felt weird to talk about it.

"Guys," Boss said, turning around. He pointed to the far bank. Dozens of Variants were charging down, screaming and howling at them.

"Keep going, Boss. Get us to the car," Ben instructed. He reached into his combat vest and slammed in a new magazine.

"Boss?" Jack said.

"Another time, Highlander." Dee grinned, her eyes twinkling in the afternoon light.

Jack returned the smile.

Boss turned. "Hey. We've been waiting for you."

"You have? Well, I would've got here a bit sooner, but I ran into a bit of bother with some locals."

Jack reached down and ruffled George's hair. "This little fighter is George. He saved me."

Dee crouched down to George. "Hey, little guy."

Jack's heart skipped a beat when the little red-haired kid wrapped his arms around her. He'd known she would like him. Perhaps, in spite of the apocalypse and the horrors they had faced, he and Dee had found that missing piece.

— 29 —

Jack could hear the howls of more monsters in the distance. Finally the river bank flattened out. Boss turned the boat for shore, heading towards a 4x4 parked under the trees.

Ben turned from scanning the bank with his scope. "All right everyone, stay frosty. We need a quick transition to the 4x4, no dawdling." He glanced at each of them. "Dee, you drive. I'm going to radio the chopper. With those pursuing Variants, that LZ is going to be hot as hell."

Jack felt the keel of the boat nudge the bank. He wrapped George in his arms and followed the others into the waiting 4x4. Jack liked this guy, Ben. The waiting vehicle was planned, the boat in the river, everything.

A chopper, coming to get us? To where? Safety?

Jack had so many questions he wanted to ask, but the ever-closer howls and screeches reminded him they had more pressing matters to be concerned about.

***

The 4x4 tore up the middle of the country road. Glancing

in her side mirrors, Dee could see the Variants closing in from the sides and rear. Urging the vehicle faster, she jammed the accelerator to the floor.

"Guys, we got company!"

A couple of Variants sprinted ahead of the chasing pack and slammed into the back of the 4x4, rocking it from side to side. Dee swerved the vehicle, but their claws tore into the metal as they tried to get a purchase.

Dee looked over at Ben. He was filling his combat vest with fresh magazines. She blinked a few times. "What should I do?"

"Just get us to the airfield. We'll take care of it," Ben said.

Ben leant out the passenger side window and tried to get a bead on the chasing pack.

Dee could still see the two Variants clinging to the back of the vehicle. "Boss, Jack, see if you can get these bastards off us!"

***

Jack twisted around in the back seat and saw the two monsters clinging on. One started smashing its head into the rear window. Tiny cracks appeared, spider webbing across the glass. With each bash of the creature's deformed skull, the cracks grew larger. Jack figured he only had a few seconds to react.

He pushed George down into the footwell. "Cover your ears."

Jack blasted the headbutting monster. The boom of the shotgun inside the small cabin rattled his brain. Jack shook his head and looked at the shattered window. The monster still clung to the back of the vehicle. Its sucker mouth seemed to be smiling as if mocking him.

It began to crawl in through the now-broken window, howling, its mouth smacking so close Jack could see the rows of tiny sharp teeth. He pulled the trigger again, this time blasting off half its head. The black gunk sprayed all over him.

Jack heard another boom of a shotgun and saw the last one fall onto the road behind them, tumbling over and over before righting itself. It started to chase them again, sprinting down the road in rabid pursuit.

Hell, these things are hard to kill.

Jack crawled into the back. Using the shotgun, he pushed the corpse out. Beyond, he could see hundreds of them chasing, moving in a weird wave as they scrambled over the fields, hunting them tirelessly.

"How much further? These bastards are gaining fast!" Jack yelled, throwing his voice over the constant rat-ta-tat of Ben's carbine.

"About half a click. It's just up over that rise," Ben said as he let off another shot. "This is going to be tight. Chopper is still ten minutes out."

Jack nodded, reached down into the ammo bag and reloaded his shotgun. He crammed extra shells into his pockets, filling them as much as he could.

After another minute, they pulled into the small airfield. Long grass surrounded it, baked dry by the hot sunny days. A small tin shed sat next to a couple of larger buildings. Jack could see a concrete pad with a big capital "H" painted in bright yellow. He scanned the sky to the west for the chopper; he could just make out a tiny speck flying out of the clouds.

***

Dee slammed on the brakes, bringing the 4x4 to a skidding halt between the buildings. She looked back down the road and saw the mass of Variants charging towards them, already down the other end of the runway. Their screeches and howls filled the air. Raising her rifle, she sighted one through her scope. Pulling the trigger, she watched as it stumbled, fell, picked itself up and kept on charging.

You've got to get these things in the bloody head!

She looked over at Ben, firing into the mass. Dee could see the odd one staying down. In that moment she realised this was it, their last stand. Unless the chopper arrived in the next few minutes, they were dead.

Dee grimaced at the thought and glanced at her husband, searching out his eyes. She wanted to look in to them and feel the love of his soul one last time. She had fought through loneliness, anger and frustration to find him. She had battled Variants, killed them, watched people get torn apart. Almost got raped.

For a few glorious moments, she had held him again.

She saw Jack grinning at her. Covered in grime, mud and Variant muck, he still looked handsome.

She could see the little red-haired boy, George, peeking out the car door, his ice-blue eyes staring at the oncoming mass. She looked over at Boss as the wisecracking teenager loaded shells into his shotgun.

Dee turned back towards the mass of monsters.

So be it, but I'm going to take down as many of you bastards as I can.

Raising her rifle back to her shoulder, Dee spotted a stack of red tin barrels off to one side, next to a large tank with a bowser attached. *Of course! AV gas! Do we have time?*

"The fuel!" Dee said, pointing. Not waiting for an answer, Dee ran over to the barrels.

Seeing what she meant, Jack and Boss followed immediately.

Dee reached up and unhooked the bowser, then depressed the trigger. Fuel started pouring out onto the grass. She sloshed it around as far as she could and watched as Jack and Boss rolled some barrels out onto the grass, straining with the weight.

"Soak the grass between the buildings. We'll burn the bastards as they funnel through."

Jack and Boss grunted with exertion.

"Monster meat is back on the menu, boys," Jack said. He unscrewed the caps, letting the high-octane fuel soak into the grass.

"Ben, how close are they?" Dee asked, sweat glistening on her forehead.

"Back in the truck everyone; they're coming up fast. We're going to have to make a run for it," Ben said, firing his rifle in short bursts.

Dee pivoted and gasped at the sight of the Variants charging towards them. Monsters as far as she could see. Howling and screeching. She pushed Jack and Boss into the 4x4 and slid behind the wheel. Thankfully she'd left it running.

Ben leant out the window and cracked open a flare. As Dee pulled away, he threw it into the pool of fuel.

The AV gas ignited instantly, spreading outwards and into the mass of Variants as they funnelled into the gap.

Many were caught in the firestorm, screeching. The smell of burnt flesh reached Dee as she glanced in the mirrors. She sneered at them twisting in pain. Burning. But for every Variant caught in the fire, dozens more were flowing around the buildings, chasing, snarling and desperate to reach them. Dee groaned and gunned the engine.

— 30 —

Jack could hear Ben yelling into a handheld radio, but he wasn't paying too much attention. He focused on the spreading fire and the rolling black mass of monsters. The fire did its job in slowing down the vanguard, giving them the precious time, they needed. Dee had driven them out into the middle of the runway. He heard Ben tell her to head for the fence surrounding the bush-clad mountain. Jack dared to have a little hope again. Having volunteered on the mountain, he knew it well. The whole mountain was surrounded by a three-metre-high pest-proof fence. Several New Zealand flightless birds, such as takahe and the North Island brown kiwi, had been reintroduced inside with great success.

The 4x4 bounced over the rough farmland towards the fence. Jack spotted the service road running along it.

"Dee, head left. There's an entry gate on that ridge."

He watched, mesmerised, as another mass of the monsters closed in from below the gate.

This is going to be close.

Jack tapped Ben's shoulder. "There's a shed next to the gate. That's where they keep some quad bikes."

Ben nodded as he gripped the door handles. "Just take

your guns. We have to hightail it up to the summit. The boys in the chopper are going to meet us there, okay?"

Everyone murmured understanding.

Jack lifted George onto the seat next to him. "Stay close to me, okay?"

"Okay."

"Don't look at them. Just run."

The mass of monsters flowed ever closer. They had perhaps a few minutes to get the bikes and go.

A chance is better than no chance at all.

***

Dee drove the 4x4 as close as she could to the gate, sliding the vehicle sideways as she stopped. She could see a small enclosure built through the fence with doors at either end. She remembered coming here with Jack when they were first dating. It was designed so only one door could be opened at any given time, a pest prevention safeguard.

Dee jumped out and, grabbing George by the hand, headed for the enclosure. She could hear the howls and screeches getting louder.

"Hurry!" Dee said, her voice full of concern.

Ben raised his rifle and fired off a few rounds. "Go! Go! Inside."

Dee didn't hesitate and pulled George through the first door. Boss and Ben followed. She could see sweat dripping off Boss as he watched the thundering mass of Variants getting closer.

"Boss. Stop gawking and move it," Dee shouted.

"All right. I'm moving," Boss said, slamming the

enclosure door shut with a clang. Dee searched around for Jack. He was still near the 4x4, struggling to get his pack over his shoulders.

"Jack! Leave it."

He looked up at her shout and turned. The Variants were only a few metres away now and closing fast.

Dee swung her rifle up and shot the first target she could. Thankfully Jack dived inside the enclosure and Boss slammed the door. Jack reached down and wedged a piece of timber through the handle as Dee and Ben continued to fire the carbines.

Dee glanced over to her husband. "Get the bikes."

Jack frowned and ran to the shed, Boss keeping close as he held onto George. Dee shook her head and refocused. She raised her borrowed rifle.

Looking through the scope at the Variants, Dee couldn't help but admire them a little. The Hemorrhage Virus had changed humans. Modified them into something else. Something almost beautiful, in an evil way. Killing machines. Perfect killing machines. The great white shark of the new world order.

Man's arrogance had finally led to his own downfall.

Dee heard engines revving in the background and fired off a few rounds as the lead monsters slammed into the fence. She lost herself in the heat of battle and held her finger down on the trigger, screaming at the beasts. It was almost impossible to distinguish between the Variants. Their mutated bodies squished against the barrier holding them out, but as more and more creatures joined the crowd, the fence began to buckle. Dee shot another monster in the head. And one through the neck. No sooner had she killed those two than four had taken their place. The Variants stomped on the dead and scrambled over the buckling fence.

Dee flicked her eyes to the retired SAS soldier fighting by her side.

He glanced at her. "There's too many of them," Ben said, worry etched on his face. "Go with the others. I'll hold them off."

Dee looked back at her husband sitting on the quad bike, George's arms wrapped around him. Boss was standing next to a second bike.

Dee slammed a fresh magazine in her AR-15. "I'm staying to fight." She breathed out and fired at another Variant, taking a chunk of jaw off with her round.

Ben chortled and joined her firing on the beasts. Side by side they fought, shell casings clinking as they hit the gravel path.

The Alpha loomed into view from the back. As it moved forwards, the other Variants moved out of the way like the Red Sea parting for Moses. The Alpha bellowed, and the constant shrieks of the creatures stopped. The silence was so sudden and complete that Dee stopped firing. She blinked and let her rifle drop.

"Keep your rifle up, soldier," Ben ordered.

Without warning, the huge Variant charged through the parted Variants. Each step he took shook the ground under Dee's feet. Out of instinct, she fired at the lumbering monster. Her 5.56 mm rounds had no effect. She might as well have been hitting it with a feather.

Ben grabbed her shoulder. "Move. Now."

Dee let Ben pull her away from the fence. She climbed onto the quad bike with Jack, little George jammed in between them.

Dee gasped, shocked, as the Alpha crashed into the gate, tearing it off its concrete footings as if it wasn't there. It stood in the now-open gateway and bellowed, a sneer spread across its deformed face.

The rest of the Variant horde reached the gap and funnelled through. Now that they weren't been fired on, the masses poured over the fence and the shrieking intensified.

"Get us out of here," Dee said. "Jack!"

Jack gunned the engine, then tore off up the track leading to the summit.

***

Jack worked his way through the gears, willing the Honda 420cc engine to go faster. His nerves were frayed beyond anything he could ever have imagined. Blissfully unaware of the virus for the first couple of days, it hadn't been until he'd reached the hut and cell phone coverage that his nightmare had begun.

The mad dash across the road-clogged countryside, his first encounter with the monsters, the family getting torn apart… His escape down the river, his capture and escape from the dam. And finding Dee, who had come to rescue him. It all flashed through his mind. He choked up at the thought. It would all be for nothing if he didn't get them up this mountain.

Shaking off the emotions, he concentrated on taking the bends of the road as fast as he could.

Jack had hiked up this mountain many times; he hoped no trees had fallen down in the high winds that buffeted the area.

We would be dead in minutes.

He urged the bike to go faster as tree branches and vines whipped over his head. Faster and faster they sped, gravel from the road flicking into the underbrush. Even over the noise of the engines running at full throttle, Jack could hear the horrific shrieks of the creatures. Thankfully the road remained clear.

George squeezed Jack's arms tighter as he took a sharp corner too fast, lifting two wheels off the ground.

"Careful!" Dee shouted above the roar of the bike.

Jack risked a glance to the side. Ben and Boss sped along behind him. This was a dash to the top, a dash to live, to fight another day.

Flying around another bend, Jack saw the stairs he was looking for. They would take them the last few metres to the lookout platform. Screeches and howls greeted him as he brought the quad bike to a stop and leapt off the bike.

"Take the kids," Dee said, lifting her rifle.

Jack nodded and grabbed George by the hand. He took the stairs two at a time, his injured leg screaming in pain. Boss bounded up ahead and, reaching the ladder, held out his hand to George. Jack looked back and gawked in horror. Variants of every size and shape spewed out of the bush.

— 31 —

Dee watched Jack, Boss and George head up the stairs. Checking her rifle, she looked back down the road. Already some of the Variants were charging towards them, their reptilian eyes fixed on her and Ben. More sprinted from the trees. First a few, before a wave of mutated humans flooded the road. Inexplicably, they stopped about a hundred metres away from Ben and Dee, as if assessing them. Dee wondered if they were contemplating which limb to rip off first.

Ben bumped into her as they backed up the stairs. She kept a bead on the massing horde. Slowly they made their way backwards until they were halfway to the platform.

"Take out the lead runners first," Ben whispered. "Aim for the centre mass."

"Okay," Dee said. She spent a few seconds taking deep breaths, trying to calm herself. To focus on the fight for life she knew was coming. She strained her ears, hoping for the sound of the helicopter.

"How long before the chopper?" she said.

"Should be here in minutes."

Dee heard a deep, angry bellow as the lumbering frame of the Alpha Variant came over the crest in the road. Bones protruding from its shoulders, it stopped and tilted its head back, shrieking. The high-pitched sound echoed around the forest, so loud it rattled Dee's teeth. She glanced at Ben, who was looking through his scope. His breaths remained steady and calm.

The huge creature moved closer, gathering the beasts with him. Now that it was closer, Dee could see the decapitated heads alongside his own. She couldn't help the shiver than ran up her spine, chilling her to her core.

So that's why they stopped. We are for you.

"Run!" Ben yelled, firing his carbine.

Dee reacted. Spinning around, she tore up the stairs towards the lookout. Ahead, the others were already clambering onto the platform. Jack yelled something to her but she couldn't hear him. Finally the sound of the helicopter came thumping through the overcast sky.

The last few days of running, fighting and surviving were catching up to her. She was emotionally and physically drained, spent. Willing her body on for one last shot at safety, Dee sprinted for the ladder. For Jack. For survival.

Jack reached down, hand outstretched, his blue eyes willing her on. She grasped his hand and let him pull her onto the platform. She scrambled to her feet and spun, searching for Ben.

***

Jack gasped in horror as the giant creature bounded up the stairs after the fleeing Ben. The soldier paused and fired a couple of bursts at the beast. The Alpha swatted away the bullets. For its size, it moved incredibly fast.

Jack had just hauled Dee up onto the platform when he heard the *thump thump thump* of the chopper. Boss was standing in the middle of the platform, waving his arms and a red flare.

Just a few moments more.

Ben reached the ladder, turning and firing over his shoulder as he went. The leader was now only metres away, his minions fanning out behind him.

Ben reached the platform and Jack rushed to help haul him over the lip. A ferocious bellow sounded out as the giant creature leapt ten metres into the air and landed on the ladder behind Ben. It pulled back one of its huge arms and speared Ben with a claw right through his side.

Ben screamed in agony as Jack tried to pull him to safety.

"Dee! Help!" Jack cried, his voice full of anguish.

Jack turned, his eyes finding Boss's. The teenager dropped the flare and rushed over. Together they wedged their feet against the railing. Ben screamed once more as they tried to pull him to safety. The beast ripped his claw free and raked it down Ben's back.

The Alpha swung his other arm at Boss, spearing him through his calf muscle. With a savage bellow and an insane glint in his eyes, he ripped off Boss's lower leg, spraying blood over the teenager. Warm, red blood arced, hitting Ben and Jack.

Thump, thump, thump.

The chopper hovered above the lookout, the wash of its spinning rotors sweeping over Jack as he hung on to Ben. The blessed sound of the minigun firing pounded in his ears. The gunner swept the blazing rounds of hot metal death at the gathering mass of creatures. The Alpha raised it arms, shaking its claws at the helicopter. Jack breathed out and, using the distraction, pulled Ben onto the platform. Frantic, he glanced at Boss. Boss was shaking and staring down at his missing leg as blood soaked the wooden planks underneath him.

Brrrrooooootttttttt.

Jack saw Dee push George towards the lowering chopper but the little boy looked back, his eyes falling on Boss and the gruesome injury.

"Take the kid and go, Jack!" Ben yelled, pain evident on his face. He winced and swung his rifle up to his shoulder. Without waiting for Jack's answer, he fired it at the beast, point blank range, until his magazine clicked empty. The beast shook his head and slammed his claw into Ben, pinning him to the platform.

Jack looked at George, conflicted. He wanted to get to safety but he didn't want to leave this man to such a horrible fate. With an angry yell, he let go of Ben's arm and reached over to pull Boss away from the Alpha. The poor kid was still shaking from the shock of his injuries.

Dee screamed as George broke loose from her grip. Pulling out the screwdriver he still had in his tool belt, George charged, screaming at the Alpha and jammed the screwdriver into its eye.

The Alpha let out a deafening bellow and released Ben.

Dee sprinted over and helped Jack pull Ben and Boss into the chopper. A man dressed in a grey flight suit jumped out and hauled the injured Boss into the hold. He said something into the mike on his helmet, but Jack wasn't paying attention, as the howls of the Variants had grown in ferocity. Dozens of them poured onto the platform as the helicopter lifted into the air.

Two Variants leapt the remaining metres and hung on to the side. Dee shot one through the head and grinned as a soldier kicked the other into the air. It flung its arms in a windmill motion before dropping out of view.

The minigun operators let loose, firing upon the Alpha, the bullets slamming into his tough bark hide. He howled up at the helicopter, swiping his huge claws at it in frustration. The gunner continued to fire. The Alpha howled once more, saliva dripping from its sucker. It jumped down from the ladder and retreated into the forest below.

Strong hands grabbed Jack, pulling him and Ben deeper into the chopper. Dazed and confused, Jack sat on the cold metal floor as the chopper soared away.

He could see monsters covering the road and stairs. They streamed out of the bush, howling up at their escaping prey. The fire still burned on the airfield, thick black smoke rising into the air. Jack let his eyes wander over the landscape and shook his head.

He was alive. He had found Dee. He had survived. He had found hope amongst the tragedy of the last couple of weeks. Jack looked over to George and couldn't help but smile at him. The little kid had saved them all. The smallest of souls can have the greatest effects.

Finally, Jack looked over at his wife. She leant against the wall of the chopper, cradling the teenager's head in her lap. One of the minigun operators was attempting to stem the flow of blood from Boss's leg. Their eyes met and they smiled at each other.

Jack found Ben's eyes; the man with the long wizard beard who had risked his life to reunite Dee with him.

"Thanks, mate. Thanks for coming to get me," Jack said. He moved over and put a reassuring hand on his shoulder.

"No one left behind, soldier. That's always been the motto. You go and be with your family, Jack."

They exchanged a look of respect, of shared experience.

Is this what all soldiers experience?

Jack nodded at the medic tending Ben's wounds. "Is he going to be okay?"

"He's losing a lot of blood. All I can do is stabilise him until we get back to base."

Jack patted the medic and slid over to Dee, taking her hand in his. He just stared at her, tears of joy, mixed with sorrow, welling in his eyes. *I made it. I found her.*

***

Dee watched Jack looking at her. No words needed to be said. They knew how lucky they were. They had survived. They had found each other amongst the chaos. Battered, bruised, wrung out, but alive.

Stroking Boss's head, she tried to reassure him. Tried to use her touch to say that it was going to be all right. She was no medical professional, but even she knew he had lost a lot of blood.

The man in army fatigues tied a strap around Boss's torn leg. "He's going to need blood, and lots of it. What blood type are you, Ma'am?" he said, adjusting the strap.

"Umm, O negative, I think," Dee replied.

"Perfect. Universal donor. I'll get set up."

Dee looked into Boss's eyes. "You hear that, kiddo?

You're going to be fine."

Boss murmured something. Dee leant closer to his lips. He kissed her cheek. "I'm Samaritan, so don't bury me in the Jewish section."

A sobbing laugh escaped Dee's lips. Even when facing death, he quoted Monty Python.

Epilogue

Jack stood on the cliff top watching the sun sink below the New Zealand mainland. The cooling salt air brushed against his healing skin.

For two weeks he had stayed in the makeshift infirmary. When they'd first arrived, the army medics and surgeon had worked through the night to save Ben and Boss. Both of them had required long surgeries and litres of blood. Dee had stood vigil next to Boss, refusing to leave his side until he was in the clear. Jack visited Ben as much as the nurses allowed; the tough old goat was sitting up in no time. Jack discovered he was a fellow WWII enthusiast. Discussions about a familiar subject had helped the healing process for them both.

Ben gave him some information about how bad it was out there in the world, while Jack told Ben of his experiences in the dam. He explained how he had made it out. They discussed the men they'd seen helping the Variants. Collaborators, Ben called them.

On the long walks Jack took to calm himself, his mind replayed how he had killed the man with the red trucker cap. Even though he had no remorse, it haunted him. He had killed someone. Snuffed out a life.

He reasoned that the man was a traitor. He'd betrayed his own kind to save his skin.

Perhaps he had deserved to die.

In Jack's opinion, they all had to band together, man against monsters. They had to stop all this petty racial bickering because they were one race. The human race. These Variants were now the apex predators.

One thing still bugged him, though. How had he and George regained consciousness when no one else in that corridor had? He mused over this for days but couldn't come up with any plausible explanation. Jack decided to let it go for now. They had bigger things to be concerned about.

Thinking of George, he smiled. George had adapted well to his new surroundings, even finding a few new friends in the camp. They had him running around squealing in no time.

Dee, Jack and George had spent the morning collecting manuka flowers from the many trees that dotted the hills surrounding the bay and camp. George had asked why they were doing this several times, and Dee had patiently explained that it was a way of remembering people. If truth be told, she and Jack had seen the ritual in a movie with Native Americans in it and had loved the sincerity of it. When Dee's father had died, she and Jack had honoured him with the ritual.

As they had no bodies to bury, this was the only way they could think of to honour those lost.

Jack and Dee had discussed at length about trying to find Jack's family. No one they knew had made it to Mayor Island nor any of the other pockets of survivors they'd had radio contact with. Jack insisted his family were smart. They knew about the cabin, so there was a chance.

Jack could feel the sea breeze picking up as it came up off the ocean and met the volcanic island. *Perfect,* he thought, smiling.

Crunching on the pathway behind him warned of people approaching. Turning, he watched in admiration as Boss, using crutches, his lower right leg bandaged at the stump, walked along behind the others.

Boss had stayed in the infirmary for a further two weeks. The nurses had finally let him out, for a short time at least.

"You guys ready?"

"Yup," they chorused.

Jack let out a nervous sigh. "We are here today to honour and remember those who we lost. We lost friends, family, pets, everything. But amongst it all, we found each other. We drew strength and courage from each other. These brave men and women on this island, and Ben, who helped us; they give us new hope so that we can carry on. We owe it to others' sacrifices that we carry on, not only for them, but for ourselves."

Jack, Dee, Boss and George raised up their arms and opened their palms, allowing the wind to carry away the crushed flowers.

Dee reached over and slid her hand into Jack's.

George clung between them, leaning out over the cliff to watch the flowers float towards the sea.

"A fine speech, Jack." Jack turned around. Frowning, he watched Ben hobble towards them. "A fine speech indeed."

Ben reached out and grasped them all in a hug.

"Benny!" George squealed.

Ben ruffled George's hair. Smiling at Jack and Dee, he nodded at each of them. "Sorry I'm late. The colonel's meetings tend to drag on. But we've a heap to do and little manpower to do it with." He stroked his long bushy beard. "Did you guys mean what you said? About letting me train you?"

"Yes. I'm keen," Jack said, looking at Dee.

She grinned. "Sure, why not."

"Good, I'm glad. We need everyone we can get. Especially people like you. You both showed real courage under fire. I think that with some training, you two will be real handy in what's to come."

"What is to come?" Jack asked.

"I can't give details yet, but we're going to fight back. The colonel's been on the horn to the Americans. That's all I can say at the moment." A pondering look flickered across his face. Jack searched his twinkling brown eyes for anything else, but Ben's face remained a calm mask.

Ben nudged Boss on the shoulder. "Boss, the colonel has agreed to teach you radio operations. He's dying to know how you reached the Americans on some amateur ham radio. You begin as soon as Doc gives you the all-clear."

Boss grinned at him, barking out a laugh. "Did I leave that part out?"

"Yes," Ben said, raising a thick eyebrow.

"You guys ever heard of a place called Guam?" Boss said. "An island?"

"A Pacific island. Yes," Ben said.

"That's where the Americans were, until I lost contact."

"There is an American base there, so it makes sense," Ben said.

Jack shifted his weight off his injured leg and chortled. He wasn't sure if Boss was joking or being serious.

Boss smirked at Dee, glanced at Jack and Ben. "You guys know I'm the hero in this rule of three, eh?"

"Hero? In the rule of three? Boss?" Jack frowned.

"Yeah, you know, teenage guy or girl ripped away from his home, orphaned. Meets old wise man. Gets trained and fights back."

"Ah, you mean the classical hero's journey. And it's twelve steps, I think," Jack said. He laughed and shook his head.

"Yeah, that's the one, but whatever."

"Kid, don't make me laugh. I'm still healing," Ben said, holding his side. "And just so you know, the rule of three is a survival guide. Basic guide at best."

Dee wrapped her arm around Boss and held him close. "You're a goofball."

Jack smiled as he turned back to see the last of the sun dip down over his homeland. Despite all the horror and trauma he had been through, he was happy. He had survived. He had escaped the Variant nest. He had saved George. Amongst all the chaos, he had found Dee. He was determined not to let this second chance go to waste. To find his family. To give George, Boss and everyone a world to live in.

He wrapped his arms around Dee, feeling her warmth as they watched the first of the stars appear on the horizon.

Not just my stars, but everyone's. They belong to everyone. To shine a little light down on this dark new world.

George squealed, the noise bouncing around the cliffs as he chased a cicada.

Jack could be forgiven for thinking everything was normal. It felt as if the last couple of weeks hadn't happened. As if Dee and he were on a camping trip, enjoying nature. Jack sighed as he looked back at the mainland. It was far from over. It had only just begun.

Three weeks without food, three days without water, three hours without shelter, and three minutes without air.

***

One Eye made his way through the field, his subjects following a short distance behind. He could smell the others approaching from the north, west and east. He stopped in the middle of the field and bellowed. Three bellows sounded out in response. They were close. Soon his plan would be put into motion. Soon the remaining humans would be corralled into nests. They needed to breed again, provide him with food.

A human fragment tugged at him. Didn't he used to do this with animals?

He shook the memory away. The anger, the hunger, gnawed at his soul. First, he wanted to find the little one who had taken his eye. He wanted to feel the satisfaction of ripping the flesh from its bones and sucking out its marrow. The humans had escaped his grasp in the thumping beast that sent stinging, burning rain on him. He had lost many of his tribe chasing them.

Finally the others approached, the Alpha leaders towering over their minions. The other three stopped around him. He looked them over. He could smell the blood as it pumped through their veins. Hear their hearts thumping. Air as it escaped their lungs.

Half of him wanted nothing more than to rip out their throats. To lap up the blood as it gushed out. To feast on their flesh until his hunger was satisfied. But he needed them. Needed their cooperation.

"Where?" he grunted, sniffing the air.

The Alpha who had come from the north signalled behind him. Variants pushed two humans, a man and a woman, forwards, shoving them to the ground at the feet of One Eye.

He gazed down at them. The blonde hair of the woman was matted against her head. He fought the urge to sink his teeth into her neck and taste her blood. The last remaining human part of his brain bubbled to the surface. *She's a real beauty.*

He bellowed angrily, then grunted, "Where?"

One of the Variants kicked the male. One Eye looked down at the slightly overweight man with his shaved head and beady eyes. He hissed at him, shoving his face closer.

"I...I...I don't know where they are, please..." mumbled the overweight man.

One Eye sniffed him. He could definitely smell them on him. He lashed out and speared the man through the head with his claw. With a satisfied hiss, he lapped up the spilling blood and brain matter.

One Eye turned to the Alpha that had come from the east. "Where?"

The Alpha pushed a skinny male out onto the ground. Skinny held up his hands in surrender, pleading, "Please...please don't kill me... I know where they are."

He pointed east, towards the mountains.

225

One Eye snarled with satisfaction. His anger barely contained, he let out a deafening bellow.

He hauled on four chains, pulling the terrified prey at the other ends towards him. Four children appeared, covered in filth. They were sobbing.

The Alphas smacked their suckers as the gathered Variants howled into the night. The small ones tasted so much sweeter.

One Eye sniffed the skull of the child in front of him and licked the salt off its flesh.

The child began to sob. With a satisfying crunch, One Eye silenced it forever. He moaned with pleasure as he drank the blood and tore into its flesh. Soon the sounds of the other Alphas feeding filled his ears.

The surrounding packs screeched and howled at the smell of the spilt blood.

END OF BOOK ONE.

Continue the adventure with

THE FOURTH PHASE

book 2 of the Extinction NZ series

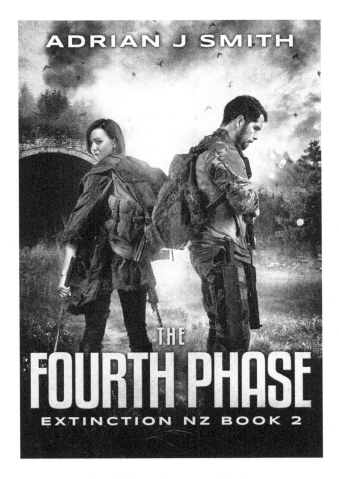

Available at Amazon Books

Glossary

Gallipoli: World War One battle fought between the ANZAC (Australia and New Zealand Army Corp) and Turkish forces in 1915. The ANZACs suffered heavy losses, but fought with sheer determination for little gain.

Haka: Tribal war dance performed to intimidate an opponent. Famously performed in modern times by New Zealand sports teams. Each tribe has its own version of the dance.

Hongi: Translates to "The breath of life." A greeting, where the two greeting each other touch noses and foreheads at the same time. Serves a similar purpose to a handshake.

Iwi: Translates to "people" or "nation", but it has come to mean tribe. In pre-European times, Maori identified more with a Hapu or sub tribe. Iwi can mean a confederation of tribes.

Kai: Simply translates to "food".

Kaitiaki: Term used for Guardianship of the Sea and of the Sky. Kaitiaki is a guardian, and the process and practices of looking after the environment.

Kaumatua: Elders in Maori society, held in high esteem. Being the storehouses of tribal knowledge, genealogy and traditions

Kawakawa: Small tree endemic to New Zealand. Used in medicines and traditional practices.

Kehua: Translates to "ghost".

Kina: A sea urchin endemic to New Zealand. Considered a delicacy.

Koru: Translates to "loop". Used to describe the unfurling frond of the silver fern. Signifies new life, growth, strength and peace.

Kumara: A species of sweet potato grown in New Zealand. Traditionally a staple food.

Maori: Indigenous population of New Zealand.

Manuka: Small flowering tree. Famed for its oily timber and, in more recent times, for the honey produced from its flowers. The honey has many beneficial properties.

Mere: Traditional Maori weapon best described as a club. Could be made from a variety of materials. Chiefs had mere made from a hard semi-precious gemstone called "pounamu".

Moriori: A peaceful indigenous people of the Chatham Islands to the west of New Zealand. Thought to have populated parts of the South Island as well.

New Zealand Flax: Endemic grass plant found throughout the country. Used for variety of reasons. Mainly for weaving traditional Maori objects. Europeans used it as a source of fibre to make ropes, etc.

Pakeha: White or fair skinned New Zealander. Specifically of European descent.

Paua: Endemic species of abalone found around the New Zealand coast.

Pohutukawa: Species of large coast dwelling tree. Often found clinging to cracks and to the side of cliffs. Called New Zealand's "Christmas tree" because its red flowers bloom in abundance during December.

Powhiri: A Maori welcoming ceremony involving, singing, dancing and finally the hongi.

Paka: An expression of annoyance or anger. Can be used in reference to a person as seen in the film *Whale Rider.*

Taiaha: A traditional Maori weapon. A close-quarters staff. Made from wood or whale bone. Used for quick, stabbing thrusts and strikes, with fast footwork by the wielder. Often found to have intricate carvings near its tip.

Tangi: A traditional funeral held on a marae (meeting place)

Ta Moko: Traditional tattoos of the Maori.

Tekoteko: Maori term for a carved human figure or head. Sometimes attached to the gable of a house.

Te Reo: The Maori language.

Whanau: An extended family or related community who live together in the same area.

About the Authors

Adrian J Smith is the author of the Extinction NZ trilogy; The Rule of Three and its sequels, The Fourth Phase and The Five Pillars.

He has had a couple of careers, He started his working life as a Painter before switching to Landscape design and construction. He switched back again, and for the last decade he has run his own successful Painting and decorating business.

Adrian lives in Hamilton, New Zealand. A self-confessed book and movie geek. He admits that he is obsessed with Star Wars, Aliens, Lord of The Rings, Harry Potter, Studio Ghibli, and Game of Thrones.

When he isn't working his day job or writing, Adrian can be found wandering the mountains, hiking, swimming, quizzing, watching movies and of course reading.

Website: AdrianJonSmith.com

Nicholas Sansbury Smith is the USA Today bestselling author of the Extinction Cycle series, Hell Divers series, the Orbs series, and the Trackers series. He worked for Iowa Homeland Security and Emergency Management in disaster mitigation before switching careers to focus on his one true passion—writing. When he isn't writing or daydreaming about the apocalypse, he enjoys running, biking, spending time with his family, and traveling the world. He is an Ironman triathlete and lives in Iowa with his wife, their dogs, and a house full of books.

Website: NicholasSansburySmith.com

Made in the USA
Middletown, DE
21 September 2019